THE LAST DAYS OF A CITY

Novel

IRMA KURTI

By IRMA KURTI

Cover Photo by Biagio Fortini
Edited by Ruth Alfar

ISBN:
Hardbound-978-621-470-175-9
MOBI/KINDLE-978-621-470-176-6
Softbound/Paperback978-621-470-177-3

Published by:
Poetry Planet Book Publishing House
Rosario, Pozorrubio, Pangasinan, Philippines
Contact Number: 09554960094
Email: maritesritumalta@gmail.com

TABLE OF CONTENTS

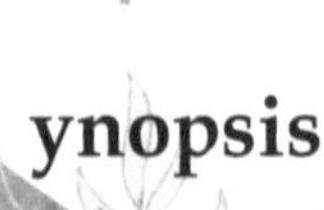

Synopsis

The story of Eva begins in deserted Bergamo, accompanied by the incessant sound of many ambulances. This city, a symbol of suffering and strength, will prove to be the perfect setting to kick off this novel.

The protagonist is a determined and sensitive woman, and her words are effective in guiding the reader through a long and profound journey between past and present, wherein the lives of the different characters mingle, merge and blend into one another. With a delicate, albeit blunt and direct style of writing, the author lays bare the protagonist's experiences, allowing the readers a glimpse into Eve's past, a past that was intense and important. The reader will thus be able to get a glimpse into this woman's life, from her childhood to adulthood.

Through wise temporal leaps and the use of different points of view, we will understand the deep bond that binds Eva to her mother Elena, the conflictual relationship between the protagonist and her brother, the emotional fragility caused by the absence of a father figure, and the strong desire to build a family where one can have a sense of belongingness.

It will be precisely this desire to create something of her own that will drive Eva to live through many experiences that will deeply mark and leave an indelible impact on her, but those will also give her the necessary strength to never lose hope. Because, as this novel demonstrates, something beautiful can always happen, even in the last pages of the book of our lives.

Manuela Raciti

To never forget those days that were drenched in agony and tears,
that separated us not only from the people in our lives,
but also from those who are no longer among us.
For my dear parents,
Hasan Kurti and Sherife Mezini,
to whom for some long months I couldn't bring flowers to
their graves and who will remain
my strength in my instants without light.

Prologue

I had no idea that day would be the last time I saw my city alive with sun and life.

People were walking down the street, while a group of kids in the park were laughing and taunting one another. Some couples hugged and kissed each other. I would have sat on a bench until sunset if I had known I wouldn't be able to see these images for a long time.

I went home, completely unaware of what was about to happen. There was no one to welcome me. My husband would be late, as usual. He is so dedicated to his job that if he had to choose between me and the job, he would almost certainly choose the latter. If he comes home earlier than usual, it isn't because he loves me. He only does it for himself. He usually rides his bike or runs around the large park about ten minutes away from our house.

He will recline on the sofa and fall asleep as soon as he finishes his dinner. When he does that, I tiptoe around the house. Our days usually end with only a few words exchanged between us.

But when I got home, he was already there, standing right in front of the oven. I tease him about working too much, and I look forward to seeing him because it makes me feel less alone. Sometimes I think he listens to me, though he has no trouble hearing.

"Eva, I'd like to speak with you," he said without even greeting me.

My blood ran cold in my veins. Something had to have happened to his family or at the plant where he worked.

THE TWO OF US

My husband's name is Diego, and he is Italian. We've been together for ten years, but it sometimes feels like we're just strangers. The beginning of our relationship was fiery. We talked a lot at first, sharing our joys and concerns, but words became scarce over time, like raindrops at the end of a storm. Our conversations helped me to learn Italian better. Oh, I forgot to tell you: I'm a foreigner who has been living in northern Italy for the past fifteen years.

Diego works as a director in a furniture manufacturing plant, whereas I, after some less than fruitful work experiences, dedicate myself to a new profession: writing.

I began writing when I lost my third job as a kindergarten support teacher. For several years, I contributed there to the development of children, but when the staff was reduced due to certain economic reasons, I was one of them. That situation compelled me to scribble down my thoughts and anxieties on paper; I had heard that this method was one of the most effective therapies. This way, I didn't have to squander the little money I'd saved by going to psychiatrists.

I'm almost done with a novel about my life. I shared some of its excerpts on social media and was successful, based on the number of likes. I plan to publish it one day. Why not? Everyone is publishing books today…

I quickly changed into a blue tracksuit, washed my hands, and sat down at the table, paying no attention to my appearance. Diego had prepared spaghetti alla carbonara. He enjoys cooking, but only on rare occasions. Who knows why he chose that evening to showcase his talent.

During that little time I had at my disposal, I considered different scenarios: Diego was planning a trip, he was laid off from work, or someone close to us was seriously ill. Obviously, as I would later discover, each of those was far from the truth.

While speaking, he didn't look at me, but at the walls of our apartment, which, to be honest, needed a do-over after many years. I swallowed hard as I followed his gaze as it wandered from one corner of the kitchen to the other.

HE FIRE HAS DIED

The news is being broadcast on television, but the volume is low. I can hardly hear what is said; they're talking about a virus that has been spreading in China, which, at the end of February has also appeared in an area 70 kilometers from where we live, Bergamo. "It's far away," I think. I had this thought months ago, when it hadn't yet arrived here. For the moment I focus on my husband's words, which seem more important for our shared fate.

Diego tells me that our relationship has recently become cold and that even our intimacy is gone (as if I didn't know).

According to him, there is no longer any love between us and that the fire has died. He wants a break so that we can both think about the future.

"I'll go to Cremona and stay at my parents' house; you can stay here or at your mom's."

"I decide where I want to go. I'm not going to my mother, and you know why," I tell him, a little nervously.

"OK, ok, stay calm!" says Diego, raising his hands in the air.

I'm silent and numb. This proposal came so unexpectedly that I wished I had listened to the entire newscast.

I nod in agreement and the only question I ask him is: "When will the break begin?"

"At the weekend," he says dryly and I feel like he has just slapped me in the face.

FEELINGS IN TURMOIL

On Saturday, March 7, Diego is in our bedroom, packing the clothes he will need in a worn-out suitcase (which is more worn-out than our relationship). I hear on the news that Lombardy has been declared a red zone, and that any migration to other cities, for whatever reason, is strictly prohibited.

The news reporter continues to speak, but her voice quickly loses clarity and begins to sound garbled. Diego must have heard the news as well, but I still went to him and told him all I'd heard.

His hand, which was holding a pair of shorts, remained suspended in the air. He shakes his head, not knowing what to do: Should he throw the thing in the suitcase or in the closet where it was before?

Finally, he places it on the bed. I like that pair of pants. He always wore it during our holidays in Rimini or at the beaches of Arcachon Bay and La Rochelle in France.

I can picture in my mind the apartment we rented in the latter city: the large table with an umbrella cover in the garden, our walks along pristine beaches while holding hands, the music from the sea shore that kept us awake until late at night, and the open window on the roof, through which I gazed at the stars with a feeling of peace and contentment. I feel a stab in my heart. How distant that time seems to me now, and how much pain it evokes in me, like the loss of a loved one.

The television continues to transmit gloomy news: "In Lombardy alone, over two thousand people are infected and the number of dead people has risen to 197."

A gray silence falls between us. Diego closes the half-empty suitcase, shakes his head, this time in dismay, and declares: "I'll stay here. Let's see how things go."

I don't say a single word and simply return to the kitchen with firm steps. I am in a state of emotional turmoil. I'm not sure if I'm worried or happy that he will continue to live at home with me.

VERY DAWN, TOGETHER

I call my mother. She lives with my brother, Alex, who, at forty, is a year younger than me. My relationship with my mum has never been stable, but it has always been influenced by my relationship with my brother.

I was twenty-five when I moved to Italy. He arrived a year later. He had no other place to go, so I welcomed him into my home. Our coexistence lasted a few weeks until he was obliged to find another solution.

I worked with an elderly woman, while he worked in a restaurant while attending cooking school at the same time. It was the first of a dozen restaurants where he would make an invaluable contribution. Our small family was then joined by our mother.

She lives in Via Corridoni, just a few minutes away from us. Actually, she is alone because my brother has gone to Spain, where a friend promised to find him a job, since Italy is going through a crisis. The truth is that my brother himself is in a deep crisis. After showing his excellent capacity as a cook in several Italian restaurants, he has now moved on to the Spanish restaurants.

Finally, my mother answers my call. I begin to explain to her that we can't leave right now because of the serious pandemic situation and that she needs to be very careful, given her age of seventy, but she cuts me off: "Do you think that I don't understand Italian at all? Do you consider me so clumsy?"

Her questions throw me off-guard so I do not respond. I'm a cool-headed person; I don't want to become angry and argue with her, so I end the call.

Diego tells me that he needs to go to the office tomorrow to get the computer, and in the meantime, he has to prepare a declaration to justify this course of action. He'll work from home, or in modern terms, he'll do *smart working*. The idea that every dawn will find us together seems strange to me. But we are not the ones who are in charge of our destiny now.

THE EMPTY BED

(ELENA)

I didn't think that one day I would migrate to Italy, away from relatives, acquaintances, and memories. But, like anything else, you grow accustomed to it, even absence, emptiness, and solitude.

My daily routine is very limited nowadays. There are no variations, no comings and goings, no visits, but then I'm not young anymore.

Usually, I sit at the bar of a supermarket near my house and meet my daughter or some friends. We just sit there for a few hours. It's as if we want to recreate the long conversations that we have over a cup of coffee in Albania. To be honest, the coffee never tastes as good as it does there. The conversations usually revolve around politics and the problems that never seem to leave that unfortunate country, a country that I feel so close to and distant from at the same time.

Eh, family? How I hope to have one!

I thought that when the children grew up, my husband, Anton, and I would finally have a peaceful life without worries, and we would devote ourselves to one another. But suddenly, things took a different turn, and I found myself unable to alter the course of events.

Years have passed since that night when Anton didn't come home, but it seems like it has just happened recently.

I was putting the kitchen in order, and every now and then, I checked on my children, who were sleeping peacefully, wrapped in the cocoon of their innocence. My husband hadn't come home yet, and it was getting very late. My waiting seemed endless. I sat on the sofa, staring blankly at the television screen, which had been turned off for some time. When it was past midnight, I entered the bedroom slowly. I felt the weight of many years on my shoulders, but more in my soul.

I had a restless sleep, full of anguish. I opened my eyes and reached out to the other side of the bed, but it was empty. It was going to remain like this even in the future.

The next morning, everything became clear to me.

CASTLE OF SAND

I got out of bed and felt numb. How could you fall asleep when you have no idea where your husband is? In recent months, he'd been working in the nearby zones and always came home every evening.

"Something could have happened to him," I thought. "A car or a truck may have hit him."

I imagined him lying on the sidewalk, people walking by, pretending not to notice him, dodging away from him as if he was an annoying object.

I wanted to start a series of phone calls to my sisters and relatives, but first I needed to put the multitude of thoughts that assailed me into order. The children were still sleeping. After an hour, I needed to wake them up as they would need to get ready for school.

I was making the double bed when I noticed the corner of an envelope tucked under the pillow. I pulled it out. On it was written: "To my wife, Elena." I recognized my husband's handwriting. It meant that nothing bad had happened to him. He had left us intentional

I didn't dare to open it. The clock on the wall ticked loudly, as if to remind me that the hour of truth was at hand. I put the envelope on the bed and didn't touch it, as if it would burn my fingers. In the end, I decided to open it. Written on a piece of paper were a few lines, and now I wished I had never read them.

His handwriting was messy, as messy as our lives in that instance.

I know this isn't the best way to say goodbye to the years we've lived together. But I'm tired of the quarrels, arguments, preoccupations, and perpetual problems in our family. I'm leaving, not to be happy, but to be at peace. Oh, I almost forgot to mention that there is a woman I have known for a while now who is always beside me. Take care of yourselves!

The letter slipped from my hands and landed on the floor. How can a man with whom you have lived with for twenty years and who is also the father of your children, get out of your life like this?

The family that I had painstakingly built over the years with plenty of sacrifices, a family that I was proud of, then reminded me of a sandcastle by the seashore. A wave destroyed it in less than a minute.

WATCH THE SUN BEHIND THE WINDOW

In the morning, I have a strange feeling of fear and anxiety, and it's an effort to get out of bed. After all, I can't go out, and I may as well spend all morning in bed.

Diego wakes up at the usual time when he leaves for work, which is before six a.m., and stays in the living room. Around eight, he asks me if I want to join him for breakfast. My heart tells me to stay in bed, but I get out of bed because I know it's for the sake of our marriage. I rush to wash my face and sit next to him, but by then he's already finished eating.

It is the eve of spring. These days are beautiful, but we can't enjoy them. The trees, motionless, resemble a painting. The sight of a few birds flying and flapping their wings reminds me that there is life and it still goes on. But now, no one can take part in it.

I start to write something like, "I watch the sun behind the window." I'm not sure what form it will take, or will it simply be an outburst of my thoughts and emotions?

In the morning, I wake up with the hope that things will get better. *Everything will be fine* is written in giant letters on the balcony of the opposite building. But when the evening comes, my hope gradually fades.

Coronavirus continues to claim victims. Every night we hear a news bulletin. More than 12,000 people have been infected, and now there have been more than a thousand deaths. Fifty doctors have been infected at the city hospital, and to think it is just a ten-minute walk from my house.

Recently, there is something which reminds me of its proximity: the ambulances that pass every five minutes with sirens blaring. That creates a state of panic inside me; I know that someone there is seriously ill, unable to breathe, and his life is hanging by a thread.

"Eva, shall I make chamomile tea?" asks Diego from the other room.

“Yeah!”

Drinking chamomile tea has now become a ritual for us. Distracted, I swirl the spoon inside the cup. In light of the recent drama of the figures transmitted by the news, the only reassuring sound is its dull and boring impact on the glass.

THE GHOST OF FEAR

Mom seems pleased on the phone; she recently talked with her dear son, my brother Alex. Even though she knows I don't really care about him, she keeps telling me about his so-called successes. He has found a job in a restaurant on the outskirts of Barcelona and is satisfied: he likes the environment, his work, and everything. Let's see how long it will last. Every job of his begins like this, with enthusiasm, then... try to guess what happens next and the ending.

Because I have no children, I'm the last person who can give advice on what a mother should be like. But looking at my mother, I realize that she has experienced more suffering than joy in life. Alex has given her many problems, but she is incapable of criticizing him. She always tries to justify his actions. She once told me, "You will understand me when you become a mother yourself." Now she doesn't say that to me anymore, perhaps because she has already understood that I will not grant her wish. As she continues to tell me about Alex, I interrupt her narration and tell her that Diego has gone to the supermarket and will leave the shopping bags in front of her apartment.

"Oh, honey, don't bother your husband, I can handle it myself."

"Mum, it seems that you are out of touch with this world. You have to stay locked up at home. How many times do I have to tell you?"

"Oh, ok, it was just to not disturb you."

I hung up the phone, and now I feel bad about my bluntness. Have I changed or have I always been like this? Can someone be transformed in just a week or ten days?

Staying at home has never worried me, but these days, my thoughts are dark, heavy, and grey. I feel as though I'm trapped in a tunnel with my husband, my mother, and thousands of other people like us. Damn! My city's name, Bergamo, is always mentioned on TV, and the situation we are in is frustrating and surreal at the same time.

One of the best moments is when I sit down to scribble something on a piece of paper or type something on the computer. I can't classify it, though, as "true writing" because I find it hard to concentrate nowadays.

The gate bell interrupts my train of thought. Diego asks me to come down and help him with the shopping bags. Although the authorities have assured us that stores and supermarkets will not close, I made a long list of things for him to buy.

"One minute," I say in a hoarse voice that doesn't sound like mine. I put on a mask and sea-colored gloves and went out.

As I walk down the stairs, not a single sound, not even a whisper, can be heard. The ghost of fear has penetrated inside the four walls of each apartment.

A LITTLE BIT, TO BE HAPPY

It seems like a typical sunny morning, but when I see the deserted streets, the buses going by without stopping because no one is waiting for them, I realize that the life we were previously accustomed to is now gone.

A few days ago, I chose to read "A Farewell to Arms" by Ernest Hemingway. At that time, I did not think of the reason behind my choice. Afterwards, I realized that the novel was perfectly suited to my current state of mind. This serious and wild situation has spiraled out of control. Many people die from the virus without being able to say "goodbye" to their loved ones or being led to their final resting place with a simple ceremony. It resembles war and all its losses, accompanied by the sense of emptiness and terror that it brings.

Diego is in the studio, and we exchange a few words every now and then. He's turned on his computer, and I can hear the tapping of his fingers on the keyboard. The sound reminds me of a woodpecker pecking on a tree trunk. He sends e-mails one after the other until he gets tired, so he opens a folder that contains photos.

Sitting on the bed, I also take a look at the photos on his PC.

He looks at them closely, as if he is seeing them for the first time. In those photos, I can distinguish our radiant faces. We're in Czestochowa, in Poland, where he asked me to marry him.

Why does he stare at them for so long? Does he regret marrying me? Or is he trying to recapture the feelings, the positivity, the dreams, the joy and the magic of that time?

After a long walk, we returned to the Mercure Hotel. Outside, a light drizzle began. I pulled back the thick orange curtains and we both looked down on the sidewalk, where people without umbrellas were hurrying towards unknown destinations. Behind the double-pane window, the scene resembled a black-and-white silent film. I turned my back on that dreary, autumn landscape.

Diego began making hot tea for both of us after asking which flavor I liked.

"Green tea," I whispered, lost, happy, and feeling drunk from the intimate atmosphere. The idea of sharing a lifetime with him seemed so perfect to me.

While we sipped tea in silence and its mist covered our faces, the rain continued to fall gently, reflecting the sentiments we felt in our souls. In the past, a little bit was enough to make us happy.

INVISIBLE (ELENA)

I can't tell exactly if, over the years, which was more disappointing: my husband's sudden departure or the fact that the more my children grew older, the more they had a stormy relationship with each other.

In moments of solitude, the pain was present and more intense. I tried to imagine the other woman, the one who stayed by his side. I try to picture her in my mind. In all cases, she didn't have straight hair, dark features, and she wasn't plump, shy, or reserved like me. She was a curly-haired blonde, somewhat on the lean side, smiling and outgoing.

When I talked with my sisters, they asked if I had noticed anything, a particular sign or clue in my husband's attitude before he went away.

"What sign are you talking about? I don't understand."

"Was he indifferent or affectionate with you?"

Anton's portrait was covered with dust, as if I hadn't lived with him for many years, but only for a few days. I saw him in my mind: tall, healthy, and smiling, with chestnut hair, black eyes, and a look that was, uhm, soft as far as I can recall.

The hectic, daily life didn't leave me time to analyze his behavior. He was travelling all the time. He worked as a truck driver and drove long distances in and out of the country. When he returned home, he was affable and he brought gifts for the children. I was sort of invisible to him, as if he didn't see me. But he, too, was like that for me. My children were my greatest love. When I was worried, they made me smile with just a tender word or a simple kiss.

But I wasn't always invisible to him. He saw me every time he wanted to vent his frustration or anger. When Alex got a low grade or when I was called to school because he played pranks on others, he didn't scold our son but me. He said it was my fault because I hadn't taught him well, especially manners.

Eva became sick one day. She had a high fever and was delirious. I was anxiously searching for an aspirin inside a drawer when Anton appeared at that moment, rudely asking me, "tell me. What have you done to our little girl?"

I didn't bother to answer. This type of conversation, with him accusing me of everything, had become normal for both of us.

I wanted our children to grow up in a quiet, family-friendly environment. I didn't want a quarrel to ensue, so I was always submissive.

For months, I thought I was the reason why he abandoned us. Maybe it was because he had instilled in my mind the idea that I was always the guilty party. The community where we belong may also have thought this way.

I had been a caring mother, but not a wife. I'd never whispered a kind word or given my hubby a loving hug.

ANGRY

Diego is losing patience. He's not used to being confined inside the house. He is used to going out, playing sports, running, and riding a bike. Now he feels caught in a trap. I saw him go to the balcony. With plenty of trees and vegetation, gardens, and swallows perched on the branches, the view is appealing. They are distant, though, and do not seem real (as if they were made of plastic) and do not evoke any real emotion.

He often initiates a conversation with a neighbor who sometimes appears on a window or balcony. They discuss the situation, but there isn't much to say or the rapport between them isn't that great. Then Diego walks into the living room, where he is greeted by the same atmosphere, the same furniture arrangement, the same air, and, finally, the same wife.

I'm curious to know if he considers this lockdown, this living together in isolation like a break, a pause for reflection. Is he still thinking about it, or has he completely forgotten?

We are now terrified, shrunken in a reality larger than us, insurmountable as a high mountain.

The latest bulletin is horrible: 368 people have died and 3590 have been infected in the last 24 hours.

We don't watch a movie; instead, we sit on the couch for hours, watching programs about the virus, the shortage of intensive care facilities in hospitals, and those sick, lonely people who desperately need to talk to someone on the phone and whose calls are unanswered. Those TV programs don't seem to mind if they instill fear or panic in their viewers. It's as if newscasters just want to say to you: "We don't care if you commit suicide. We are only interested in making our programs as riveting as possible".

As I listen to the news, I find myself being transformed into another person: cold, icy, and impenetrable.

"What are you thinking?" Diego asks me, "You seem angry."

"I'm just sad."

I am shocked by the number of victims, which continues to increase, and by the situation that is becoming more and more suffocating. I may also be angry because the area where we live has the highest number of infections, or maybe because this virus has completely disrupted our lives. But I keep these thoughts to myself and, with firm steps, I go over to the microwave oven to heat my chamomile tea. At least nobody can take my chamomile tea away from me, whose sole duty is to reduce my anxieties and help me sleep.

THE ACQUAINTANCE WITH DIEGO

At a period where a few acquaintances couldn't be transformed into a relationship, I didn't care much about having a social life.

In the evenings, I sat in front of my computer and chatted with strangers, desperate people like me, who may be looking for a soul mate (or maybe not). I was simply looking for someone to talk to, so as not to feel alone. Conversations with them were superficial and futile. The next day, I couldn't even remember their names or nicknames.

One day, I met Diego online. We chatted in the evenings and then exchanged phone numbers. Months passed by before we actually saw each other because he lived far away from me.

Diego was a tall man with a muscular body; he had curly hair, black eyes, and a good sense of humor. I wasn't fascinated by his muscles or his passion for physical activity, because if it were up to

me, I wouldn't even want to go out of the house. I don't like walking at a fast pace for miles, and I don't even want to hear the word "gym."
I was attracted to his smile, his ability to inject humor into everything and thus minimize the seriousness of certain problems.

I am like my mother: I'm reserved and I hardly talk to strangers (except those behind the computer screen), while Diego will even start a conversation with the stones on the road if he chooses to do so. Working as a waitress, though, helped me to stay fit, so I was pretty thin. I always kept my hair long because going to the hairdresser cost too much.

When I asked Diego what he liked about me, he was evasive, staring into space as if he would find the answer out there. He told me he couldn't define it. He said that when he saw me, he just had the desire to know me better and meet me again. It wasn't what I wanted to hear, so I repeated this question again and again over the years, but his answer always remained unchanged.

We both shared a passion for traveling and visiting new places, having fun and living a good life, but I didn't know the reason why love remained elusive.

N THE FIRST PAGE OF A NEWSPAPER

I knew of someone in my hometown who tainted my image of love. It was the first time I felt that way, but that person gave me so much disappointment that afterwards I began to fear love as much as I feared the devil.

One of the most beautiful and poignant memories I have is of our walks hand in hand along the lake shore. We were so innocent at that time. However, it wasn't long before I saw Fabio transform into someone I didn't know—a stranger. I was 21 then, and he was four years older.

He was a handsome blond with green eyes, and with him I felt that I was living a dream life. He didn't have a job, but he always seemed busy. He did all kinds of work, but I didn't know exactly what it was. I would discover that later.

I wasn't afraid of anything when we were together; I ignored all the gossip that was circulating in our neighborhood.

A few months later, he just disappeared. The walks, the melody of the waves, the seagulls flying above us, the panorama of the beach that we saw in our minds as we kissed each other with eyes closed---all of those became distant memories.

We often met in secret, in suburban bars where there were only a few people or just the two of us. According to him, it was necessary so as not to create problems with my family, particularly with my brother. The latter had to grow up too soon. He took on the role of being the man of the house, assuming the responsibilities of a father who had abandoned us when we were just kids.

Alex controlled all of my movements. He wouldn't let me date someone he didn't know and who was certainly involved in some sort of shady business. He told me he had seen my boyfriend with other girls, but when I confronted Fabio about this, he got angry and raised his voice, telling me that I was the only one for him.

But then, even Fabio controlled all of my movements. Every time I went out with a friend, I had to ask his permission and get his approval. Sometimes, when I couldn't answer or miss some of his calls, he would disappear for days, as a form of "revenge". This kind of relationship went on for almost three years.

Alex came home one day, slamming the door behind him and muttering something through clenched teeth. I was lying on my bed reading a magazine when he suddenly appeared at the threshold. I barely looked at him, engrossed in my reading.

"I told you a hundred times not to go out with that scoundrel!"

"I also told you to leave me alone, for I'm not a child."

At that moment, mom showed up. Her face was pale, and she looked tired. She begged us not to shout because the neighbors could hear us.

"Read what has been written about your prince charming and open your eyes," Alex said, throwing a newspaper at me.

I caught it, but had no intention of leafing through it in his presence.

"Just think, because you are much too naive for your own good!"

"Go away. You're so annoying."

My brother left. With trembling fingers, I was about to leaf through the newspaper, but it wasn't necessary after all. Fabio's picture was on the front page. The photo was in black and white, but he still looked as handsome and attractive when I first met him. There was a caption written below the photo: *Fabio G., the leader of an armed gang, was arrested today by the police.*

My heart was beating fast, and, strangely enough, all my worries and sorrows dominated the circumstance of having discovered my "love's" true nature.

OUR GAZES

I was 11 when my father left us, so I remember very little about him. I can remember the gifts he brought home from his travels abroad, the empty Coca-Cola or Fanta bottles that we kept in the closet; the t-shirts with various images printed on them. They were my pride because no other child had them.

I was cheerful because my parents loved me and I thought that happiness would accompany me all the way. I also thought that adults were always happy too. Mom never complained, while Dad laughed and joked every time he took us in his arms when we went to the beach or walked together.

On the sand and under the heat of the sun, he played with us as if he were a child himself. He had fun with the ball, dug holes using plastic shovels and filled those holes with water. When he went to the sea, he took me with him. Alex stayed with mum. Together, we went deep into the water. I clung to his shoulders and, with the other hand, drove the waves away, as if dispelling them. It seemed to me that I was swimming when I did that. Dad swam by opening his large and powerful arms like an eagle. His breathing was loud and he blew hundreds of water bubbles. This image I had of him was so vivid and real that it just seemed natural that he would always be close to me, guiding me along the difficult paths amidst the waves, until I learned to swim by myself.

I didn't know which part of the script prompted me to think that things weren't going well. It must have been when I saw my mother's melancholic gazes and pondered on her uneasy silence. Perhaps that's when I realized that my father had abandoned us. There was a huge change in our daily routine, but to top it all off, I began to suffer in solitude. That pain eventually became an inseparable part of me.

At first, my mom told me that Dad would be back eventually, but after some time, she would no longer answer my questions. She deflected my queries, telling me that the most important thing was that she would always be with me and Alex.

She had found a job, but in the afternoons she always felt tired and unenthusiastic. Without saying a word, she would wrap us in her arms and in that embrace, we were a family, united and strong in the face of adversity. After the hug ended, each of us felt alone, or rather, we felt dad's absence. Our mother suffered much. Years later, she would tell me that what hurt her the most was not her husband leaving, but the fact that he had another woman by his side. This made her feel guilty for not giving the best of herself in that relationship.

I remembered my dad coming home with his hands full of presents. He brought me much happiness and joy. When I never saw him again, I found it hard to imagine how he could turn his back on us. My mother's eyes often became pensive; she kept glancing at the door, as if at any moment it would open and dad would be there. Our gazes were directed at the door. But my father never appeared at that threshold ever again.

THE SLAP (ELENA)

I never thought that one day I would miss some of the things that I had taken for granted in the past, such as a walk in the park, a coffee at the bar, or a hug from friends. Now, only the phone calls with my children and relatives from Albania have remained as my life's little pleasures. The name of our city has become so popular that even relatives I hadn't heard of before have called or texted me. They heard the news and are concerned. They ask us how we feel, but our feelings are too difficult to express in words.

I feel sorry for Alex. Things are not going well for him up to this point. He went to Spain because here he couldn't find a job with a good employment contract, but then the damn virus also reached there, so all of their restaurants were temporarily closed.

My honey, you have been unfortunate your whole life!

Eva tells me that she had no doubts that things would happen like this, but I choose not to listen to her. How harsh she is on him! But I understand her; she has her reasons for being so.

When we sat down for a drink, I couldn't even begin to mention Alex's name. She prefers to stay away from trouble and lead a quiet existence, but is this possible when it comes to a family member?

When my husband left, I was alone with my two children and received no financial support from him. I don't need to hide this truth. My sisters supported us until I started working.

Although Alex was only a year younger than his sister, he erased his father's image from his mind, whereas Eva kept asking questions. At first, I was too tired to give her detailed explanations. I was angry with my husband and with what destiny had served us. I just told her that her dad was on a long journey and would soon be back. I don't know why, but I chose to believe this fable too.

Months passed and my daughter had grown silent. She kept touching her father's gifts, the only real things that bound him to her memory. I thought that once she grew up, that void would be gone, but then she still seemed lost, with a questioning look that remained even when she reached adulthood. In their father's absence, Alex became strict and controlling, as if he took it upon himself to assume an important role: to replace his father. He wanted to have the last say on everything and wanted to keep things under control.

One evening, Eva came home late; she looked happy, her eyes sparkled, and her cheeks had taken on a rosy hue. Who knows what pretty lies her boyfriend told her? I went into the living room and heard Alex's angry voice.

"You are always on the streets. Where were you until now?"

"You are still young to ask me this. You have to grow up first."

Suddenly, I heard a noise and went quickly towards the corridor. My daughter was rubbing her cheek with her hand and tears were rolling down her face. In an instant, her joy was shattered into thousands of pieces.

"You shouldn't have done that, son!"

"Mum, leave me alone!"

One slap was all it took to break the fragile relationship that existed between them.

LIFE BY A DROPPER

Nowadays, we don't care about the weather forecasts. Before, we kept track of them: on television, radio, and, to be sure, even on our mobile phones. Now that we are locked up at home, it doesn't matter if the weather is nice or rainy, warm or cold.

But as if to mock us because it is impossible for us to go out, the days continue to be sunny and the sky is bluer than ever.

Diego goes out to the balcony and looks at the sky. Surely, he must think of clouds and rain like me. Then we would be satisfied and this prison would make sense.

In the afternoons, people went out onto the balconies or windows and started singing, exchanging kind words and smiles to express mutual solidarity. I saw all of that on TV, because here in my area, nobody did those things. I didn't see any faces behind the glass, nor a single movement of the curtains. This city has been covered with pain and has no voice or heart to sing or smile, to say that everything will be fine. It can't be fine if thousands of people have died. Perhaps it is even the proximity to the hospital, that ambulance siren is heard every minute - day and night - that reinforces this thought.

I don't know if this lockdown will have any influence on us; if after this we will become better, more sensitive, and more inclined to help each other, or if we will move further away from each other, to continue another type of isolation, the mental one. One thing is certain: it allows us to reflect on our daily lives, on our often-misguided choices, lifestyles, and priorities.

How will Diego and I get out of this predicament? It's a question I ask myself from time to time. But the situation in which we find ourselves worries me; therefore, I live life moment by moment, little by little, as if it were offered to me by a dropper.

A VACATION IN TUSCANY

I can't remember the exact year, but it was September when Diego and I went to Pisa, in Tuscany, with another couple. We rented a villa outside the city. It had two floors: the first was the kitchen, and in the second, there were a few rooms with tiny wooden windows. In front of the villa, there was immense greenery. There were no other houses nearby, so we were completely isolated. We returned to the house late in the afternoon after visiting other touristic localities.

After dinner, we rested, talking for hours as the cold breeze chilled our skins. We drank beer and ate potato chips, planning other trips that we would take in the future together. However, that remained the only trip the four of us made.

Silence surrounded us. Only the faint sound of a cricket or the timid flapping of a nocturnal bird could be heard. Diego and I felt happy and carefree. When he was with friends, he had plenty of topics and trivia to talk about. I needed tranquility, and I thought I had found it. But then I realized that I could never be totally at peace since the ghosts of the past (which I thought were buried deep inside of me) suddenly reared their ugly heads and disturbed my peace of mind.

Our friend's partner, Giada, loved physical activity; she was agile, had a lithe, slender body, and was quite a chatty person. She told Diego that the two of them had many things in common: their love for sports, walking, running, and other physical activities. She often joked with him and they laughed together, while I felt awkward and uncomfortable.

If I were made to stay in a house that was near the sea or surrounded by lush vegetation, I would be happy to stay there. For an entire day, I would be content to read books or write something. Thus, it seemed that Diego and I had nothing in common. I heard those exact words coming out of Giada's mouth. I was filled with rage, but then I tried to restrain myself. We were there to rest and not to argue with one another.

Diego got up early the next morning to take a walk in the woods, and Giada joined him. I didn't go out of the room. Beyond the window pane, I stared at a pine tree that swayed with the breeze, wondering in which part of the forest they were at that precise moment. All kinds of dreadful scenarios filled my head: of Giada seducing my husband, throwing her arms around his neck, then eloping with him, thus leaving me alone.

I remembered my mother, who, one morning, had found a letter in which my father wrote that he was leaving her for another woman. She transformed her frustration into strength so that she could raise us properly and provide for our education. For many years, she tried to imagine what that other woman looked like; she appeared in her dreams and there, my mom vented her rage at the person who had destroyed her family. As years went by, however, she didn't feel resentment anymore and seemed to have accepted her fate.

When they came back from their walk, I carefully scrutinized his face to see if his lips were redder than usual or if there were any other telltale signs telling me that something had happened between them.

I felt tense and anxious all day long, acting cold and distant towards Diego; I didn't enjoy the walks by the sea, the colorful sight of umbrellas lined up in a pretty manner, or the sight of a few vacationers soaking up the last rays of the sun. I only thought of their walk. Now and then I try to say something to my husband, but what?

"You seem strange. What happened?"

"Oh, nothing."

I didn't want to tell him how I really felt because he would just say that I was jealous. For how long was I going to hide my insecurities?

Dinner found us outside, as usual, gathered around the large table.

"I want to ask you a question, but be honest," Giada addressed her statement to Diego, and just then I jumped, as if a snake had bitten me.

"Listen," I said. "It's dark and you are probably confused. This one here is my husband, not yours."

After saying those words, I kissed Diego with passion, not because I really felt it, but out of spite.

Under the dim light of a lamp that was suspended from the red tiles of the roof, Giada stared at me, as if she wanted to eat me alive. She tried to say something, but then she changed her mind. Her question remained suspended in the air, unspoken even until now.

I was not bothered that she felt bad. What surprised me was myself. I thought that memories and joys, but not strong feelings, bound me to Diego. I had overcome my shyness, fear, and insecurity. I had let out the monster I kept inside of me. Was it because of jealousy or love? Was it my unhappy past that had prompted me to do things?

Maybe we don't realize how much we love someone until we face the risk of losing him.

THE DAY DOESN'T BELONG TO ME

My days are not the same. Maybe because they are often long and the moments change continuously. Sometimes they are monotonous, sometimes sad or hopeful. Oftentimes, positive thoughts refuse to stay with me.

Diego no longer listens to the news or programs that talk about the virus. He says that they disturb him and won't let him sleep. But is this a solution? We can't ignore the sirens, we just can't ignore this situation. And I thought that he was brave, a safe harbor where I could take refuge from my fears.

I can't stay in bed, but I don't want to get up either. I walk around the house as if I have lost my sense of direction. I go out on the balcony and see the motionless trees, the absence of a passer-by, of a child, of a car.

This emptiness suffocates me.

I enter the studio, connect to the internet, and read a title written in capital letters: Bergamo mourns its 385 deaths in a week.

I want to cry and scream too, but I can't. I feel numb and depressed.

This beautiful, sunny day does not hold any fascination for me, does not belong to me. It is gloomy and sad for me because of the news and the sirens of the ambulances. You understand that somewhere, a life, or many lives, are struggling to breathe, are in serious condition, and may not win the battle against the virus.

This is war. Surely, we'll win in the end, but at what cost?

Shocking photos of dozens of coffins lined up in the cemetery church have been posted on the social network. My city has lost its smile.

We finish lunch. I clear the table and go to the other room when Diego calls me.

"Eva, let's watch this movie together if you want to. It has just started. It is with an actress you like: Jamie Lee Curtis."

It amazes me that he remembers such a detail. However, before I can say anything, his cell phone rings and the words get stuck in my throat. Diego answers, and he just listens. Then he murmurs, in a low voice, "Yes, I understand."

He slowly walks down the corridor. Then he comes back. His curly grey hair seemed frazzled, as if he had been running his fingers over it. His slightly aquiline nose looks smaller. He blinks fast and seems upset. Finally, he hangs up.

"What's the matter?"

"My aunt Maria, who had been in a nursing home for a number of years, died. Half of the elderly people there have been infected with the virus and so far the victims are thirty."

"I'm sorry. I remember her well. We met her at home a few years ago."

"I am sad that I can't go to her funeral. I loved her because she was a fantastic person! My aunt does not deserve this fate."

"Nobody deserves this fate."

We sit on the sofa like robots, motionless and staring blankly into space. We stop watching the film. We have lost track of its storyline anyway. Our existence has now become difficult. Life these days is like a thread that can snap or break anytime.

ILLUSIONS

I was home alone that afternoon. I didn't feel relaxed in the presence of my brother because I couldn't do the things I liked.

He always criticized me.

I didn't know how long I kept staring at my boyfriend's photo in the newspaper. At first, I thought it was just a mistake: it couldn't be true that the person I had known for more than two years was the leader of a street gang. But when the television news continued to talk about the arrests, mentioning Fabio's name, I wanted to go far away and become invisible.

I took a pair of scissors and cut out the article, folded it, and put it in the nightstand drawer. I wanted to keep it as a souvenir. The guy who had made my heart beat fast, who was the embodiment of love for me, had been a deceiver. A part of me felt sorry that he had ended up in prison; the other part felt anger and indignation.

How was it possible that I didn't notice all the signs before? His disappearance every now and then, the fact that even without a job, he had a lot of money and gave me expensive gifts, the rumours that circulated about him...

I had been blind. Alex had told me these things, but then our relationship was really tumultuous. I would never thank him for opening my eyes. He was unyielding and aggressive, as if I were not his sister, but someone who had dishonored his family.

Several days passed before I got a call from Fabio. When I heard his voice, I was overwhelmed by a sudden wave of emotion. Nothing bad had happened—that gloomy news did not exist. It was just the two of us and our love.

"I'm calling you from prison," he said, and all of my illusions and expectations vanished in an instant. "Don't worry, everything will be fine. Soon, we'll be together again."

"I had a feeling it wasn't true."

"You're right. I'm not the gang leader."

"So you're not involved with them?"

"I'm just a gang member. I've done everything for you and us to have a better, worry-free life. Otherwise, we'll be like our parents, who worked and sacrificed so much for a lifetime, yet in the end....

I didn't want to listen to him anymore. I was tired of this story. And as he went on talking about love and our bright future, a thought flashed through my mind like lightning, yet I didn't have the courage to say it out loud: "There is no more *us,* dear Fabio."

THE CRUMPLED ENVELOPE

My boyfriend didn't call me anymore, and this made me feel better. The distance and the lack of communication will eventually break us up anyway. That person didn't deserve my love.

Days passed peacefully yet troublingly. I couldn't accept that fate had led my path straight to him.

I continued to work in a call center, and with my salary, I helped my family because we were in financial crisis.

One day, Mom seemed worried.

"Is something going on?" I asked her. She didn't answer but led me towards the small room. She opened the wardrobe, and there, among her clothes, she searched for something: an envelope. It was crumpled, as if it had come a long way to reach us.

"This is a letter for you."

I wondered why she was so dramatic with her actions. When I looked at the envelope, Fabio's almost illegible handwriting caught my eye: the letters were spaced closely together, almost as if they were afraid of falling. Our home address was written with errors.

"Is Alex home?"

"Not at all. If he had this in his hands, he would have surely torn it to shreds. Why do you still communicate with that impostor?"

"I'm done with him."

Mom had her hair pulled back into a ponytail and seemed pretty, almost like a teenager. It was a shame that Dad hadn't been able to recognize her beauty.

She calmed down when she heard those words. She hugged me and held me for a long time in her arms. Then, as if she remembered something, she pulled away from me and asked: "What are these letters then?"

"He doesn't know yet, but soon I'll tell him that I don't want him in my life anymore."

I don't know how to say this to my boyfriend.

A LETTER FROM PRISON

Dear Eva,

Every morning when you go to work, I see you. I would like to be with you and walk along the road together, but I know that, for now, this is not possible.

I have made mistakes in the past. I had to stay close to you to help you with family problems. But I'll prove to you one of these days that I can be a better person than the one you know. I am convinced that you will wait for me even if this situation lasts for a long time, because love surpasses all difficulties.

Soon, I will get out of this cell where the sun's rays can't reach. I promise. We live in a country where you can always find a way out of things. I have saved enough money in order to survive situations like this.

When I get out of here, we'll take the trip you wanted so badly. In Paris! Do you remember that it was your dream? Then it became mine too, but my work did not give me enough free time to make it come true.

Perhaps you were surprised by what I wrote at the start of the letter. Let me tell you that it's not me who is following you. I wish it was me, but then it's a friend of mine. I told him to watch over you, to see to it that no one harasses you, because we live in difficult times.

They think that by arresting me or someone else, they are destroying us, but they will never succeed. You know why? There are many of us in every city, in every area, north or south. Our bonds are strong, and they cannot be easily severed as you can with a pair of scissors.

You are in my thoughts and I ask this of you: don't forget me! You will be mine and nobody else's!

I'm waiting for an answer.

Yours, forever, Fabio.

FRAGILITY

I have not received any response from you and, to be honest, I don't know what's on your mind. Are you angry because I didn't tell you the nature of my job? It's understandable. How could I tell you? You would be afraid and leave me. And I don't want that to happen.

You must be proud that I love you, because I have never lacked for girls, some even more beautiful than you. I am not saying this out of spite, but to emphasize the sincerity of my feelings. The important thing is that I always came back to you. I also stayed next to you for another reason: to show your brother that our relationship was not just an escapade, as he thought.

I knew your misgivings, those that were deeply rooted in your mind. I felt that you lived with the fear that sooner or later I would abandon you for another. I can't forget the uncertainty that I read in your eyes when we met after a few days or after a week and you thought I would tell you that our relationship was over.

You must appreciate the fact that I didn't leave you. I was sorry for you. I wanted to protect you from this world. I think you know all of these, so I can't understand your silence.

Do you really think you can get rid of me? You can't just abandon me in difficult times when I need love.

I'll wait for your letter.

OU WILL BE MINE

Are you alive? You have to know that this behaviour of yours irritates me. You think I'm helpless inside this cell and there's nothing I can do about it. As I said to you before, I am inside but also outside.

I have friends with whom I have had my share of adventures, those challenging moments when our adrenaline levels were at their peak and we didn't know whether we could return home or not. These are friends I've met in my line of work. I could instruct any of them to remind you to drop me a line.

Is it possible that you don't think of me anymore? Presumably, you loved me very much. Or are you like some other girls who are fickle and don't have a sense of loyalty? They, who are so much like each other except by name?

The days pass by slowly. There are many others like me in here, but at least they have relatives who visit them once in a while. Nobody visits me, not even my family, because I've brought shame to them. They didn't know that a monster lived among them. Other parents are able to accept their children's faults, but mine can't. Tell me, is this love? Simply put, you're doing exactly the same thing.

Do you remember the lunches and dinners in nice restaurants? And the expensive clothes? Tell me, did you like them?

I thought I was going to kill time here by reading your letters. But since you are either too lazy to write to me or maybe you just don't want to, I will not say "Go to hell," because I'm an educated person. I'll just say, "Do what you want."

PS: You will be mine and nobody else's!

MARIONETTE

Fabio's letters destroyed my peace of mind. When I didn't receive any letters from him, I felt free. I fooled myself with the illusion that he had forgotten me. I didn't think love was the reason why he kept on pursuing me, but anger and resentment. The fact that a girl chose to ignore him with silence and indifference made him angry.

His tone varied with every letter. He wasn't gentle anymore; instead, he became harsh and aggressive. He tried to make me feel guilty by mentioning the occasional dinners at expensive restaurants or some birthday presents he gave me. The guy whom I loved and with whom I had planned a future with—where had he gone?

Mom understood that I was going through hell. She also felt helpless. She was caught in the crossfire between me and Alex. As soon as my name was mentioned, he got upset or angry because he was ashamed of me. He was sure that I still had communication with "that prisoner" and nothing could make him change his mind. When he was home, I didn't go near Mom and talk freely with her, because he was rude to us, a kind of dictator. He controlled our lives as well as our conversations.

My brother's youth vanished into thin air. I didn't even see him smile anymore. He was always gloomy and quarrelsome. When I was a child, I was glad that we were more or less the same age. I considered him more of a friend than a brother. I didn't think that one day I would avoid him or be afraid of him. Was it our father's absence that had transformed him? Was he really weaker than me? He, who appeared to be strong and invincible? Was he more insecure than me? Would he soften up a bit if he had a girl by his side?

My days weren't the same. Sometimes, I felt like a marionette in my boyfriend's hands. He had control of my mood even though he was locked up in a cell, which to my imagination was small, dark, and damp. And this would go on indefinitely until one morning....

THE STRANGE ENCOUNTER

People were hurriedly walking down the street to get to work. I didn't know why I was thinking about my dad that morning; it was like he would suddenly appear out of nowhere and talk to me. I'm sure I wouldn't recognize him. What traces would he have left on his face? Did his hair turn gray? Was he still that handsome man I remembered from childhood?

I was thinking along those lines that when someone called my name, I really thought it was my father. I turned my head and I still had a smile on my face, not knowing that this was the last thing I would like to give to the person in front of me.

He was a very thin, young boy, looking like he was about to faint. He had pale skin and was sporting a ponytail. He was not the kind of person I would know, so I went on walking, thinking that my ears must have been playing tricks on me. He raised his hand in the air and said to me, "I have something to say to you."

I stopped, and my quickening heartbeat was a warning that this wouldn't be a pleasant encounter.

"I'm friends with your husband, Fabio."

"Excuse me, but I am not married."

"That doesn't matter. I've been watching you for some time at the instruction of the boss. I saw you passing here one day with a friend of yours. Who was he?"

"I don't need to give an account of what I do to a stranger."

He grabbed my hand and pulled it hard.

"I believe I introduced myself. It is you who's being impolite. I won't tell him anything today, but you must know that next time I'll tell him the truth. So be careful!"

He raised his middle finger at me and grinned, his yellow and rotting teeth coming into view. I felt sick to my stomach.

I walked away quickly. I was so upset that I missed the alley where my office was located. I was restless and nervous. During calls, I was confused and anxious, as if it were my first day at work.

A feeling of panic then engulfed me. I had thought that since Fabio was in prison, I would be free to live my life, to choose another path without him. But that wasn't the case after all.

When I got home, I felt an urgent need to tell Mom about what happened. She was the only person I could talk to about this without feeling guilty.

"Mom, I need to talk to you."

"Me too, sweetheart."

We both sat down on the sofa. I could see the first signs of wrinkles on her face. I felt shame upon seeing those lines on her face, often thinking that I was the cause of those wrinkles.

I told her about the strange encounter that morning, adding that in this city I could never find another love nor create a family.

Mother said, "I have always wished and dreamt that at least you would have a peaceful and happy life, with a family of your own."

She took my hand in hers and caressed it as she did when I was a child.

"And you, what did you want to tell me?"

"Recently, the phone has been ringing a lot, but no one has spoken from the other side, but today someone did."

"Who was it?"

"He didn't tell me what his name was. He only said, "Tell your whore daughter to be careful, otherwise we will set your house on fire."

"It seems like I'm the one in prison and not him. I can't do anything else aside from going to work. Who knows if tomorrow he will also stop me from going to work?"

"Try not to worry. We'll talk about it tomorrow when we are more relaxed. Let me hug you."

In my mother's arms, I felt safe and protected from all the evils of the world, but above all, I felt free, like I was walking through an oasis, a peaceful place where a lot of people smiled, where there were children running, holding white flowers in their hands.

SMALL FAMILY, BIG PROBLEMS

The first trip I took with Diego was to Como. We had just known each other and this new adventure, coupled with the anticipation of what this city had to offer, made us excited. We talked incessantly along the way; we had a lot to tell each other, and I remember those moments with nostalgia.

When we arrived, we struggled to find a parking space, and then we had to wait in line to get tickets for the ferry trip around the lake. We weren't intimate yet, but we walked hand in hand as if we had known each other for a lifetime. We looked at the villas surrounded by greenery, the buildings on the shore of the lake, and the boats swaying in the light breeze coming from the west.

We stopped at Bellagio. A light mist covered the lake, and the seagulls behind that layer of mist seemed to be protected from some impending storm.

I had no idea how far we had walked before we sat down to have an aperitif in one of the many bars that lined several of the city's narrow streets.

I told him some sad events from my past, memories with my parents or my brother, Alex, while Diego told me about a long and tiring relationship with a girl who had taken away the best years of his youth.

"I thought the feeling would grow stronger, but it was losing its magic every day," he told me.

The fact that he didn't ask me anything about my past was a puzzle to me. Didn't he care about me or was he bored with my stories, which almost always have the same unhappy endings? Did he sense that I was a reserved person?

I can't say for sure if I was ready to open my heart and tell him the details of a relationship that had robbed me of the desire to find love again.

Sometimes I couldn't understand myself. I wanted to share the story of my life, with all its pain and sadness, only with the person who would be with me for the rest of my life. Why all this persistence to hide a past that nobody cared about anyway? What would happen if....

The ringing of the phone interrupts my thoughts. It's my mom, Elena. Her voice brings me back to reality.

"My sweetheart, I'm worried."

I gasped when I heard her frightened voice. "She is infected with the virus," I thought.

"One second, I'll go to the other room."

Because my relationship with Diego is going through a rough patch, I don't want to involve him in the issues of my small family, which has big problems.

IALOGUE

"Mom, how are you?" I asked her, my heart beating fast.

"I'm fine, but Alex..."

How many more days, months, or years will my brother disrupt my peace? I had told her that I didn't want to hear about him anymore. I wanted to say it again for the thousandth time, but I held back my tongue.

She is living alone now, which is sad, and she certainly must be under pressure from this situation. I shouldn't vent my anger on her either. Gritting my teeth, I ask her casually, "Why, what happened to him?"

Thank God, he's fine. He's only run out of money. They weren't able to give him his first salary because a state of emergency was also declared there.

"What do you want from me? I don't understand."

Silence.

"He's very upset. He wants to come back here, but the airports are closed and he feels trapped."

"Maybe they'll let him come in a private plane. An important person like him deserves that."

"Eva, I'm worried."

"Yeah, well, I got it. I don't know what I can do in the meantime."

"Um... you can help me. This is what you can do. I would like to send him five hundred euros, but everything is closed and the only way is by bank transfer. You know I'm not practical because I'm an old woman now. "

"Go on, keep giving that parasite money."

"Honey, he is in trouble. Don't you understand the situation he's in?"

"Who knows why these situations always happen to him?"

"Will you please help me? Can you send him those euros?"

"I've told you a hundred times that I don't want to be involved with him."

"Talk to Diego and reach an agreement with him. Then I'll give you the money."

"I don't understand your point."

"I'm begging you, my daughter! I don't want him to suffer. He is still your brother."

"Ugh!"

I wanted to scream out the hatred that I keep inside, hang up my cell phone, get out from the four walls of this house, cut off all ties with my family and with my husband. Be free from everyone, because they will only make me worry, making my life difficult.

"Eva, are you there?"

"Okay, Mom, I'll talk to Diego and make the transfer."

"Ah, honey. I know you have a kind soul. I love you so much!"

A WOMAN'S HEART (ELENA)

When my husband left me, I had two children, aged 11 and 10, and still hadn't given up on dreams. I missed the things we did together: walks by the lake, games on the beach with our children, going to the pastry shop, or even a sudden hug during a conversation. I miss hundreds of little things, which previously seemed like just a normal part of my daily routine.

I wanted my children to grow up happy, have a peaceful life, finish their education, then find work and have a family. With a little bit of luck, I would also become a grandmother.

When Anton was still with us, every obstacle seemed surmountable; when he went away, my life was filled with questions. I felt scared and all alone.

During the first few months, my family stood by me. When I found work taking care of a child not far from home, the shock I had felt at first began to subside.

The years passed and I got used to not locking the door in the hope that he would appear at any moment and we would return to our old life. I liked to think that he was going on a long journey. All my emotions—the anger, hatred, and resentment—were fading away. I tried to understand him, to find the reasons behind his departure. He was a man I had known for twenty years, my first love and most certainly my last.

Perhaps he had found another woman more beautiful than I am, who said kind and loving words to him, touched and complimented him, things I wasn't able to do. However, I couldn't understand how he could abandon our children. He was the one who came back with his hands full of gifts, who played with them like their friends, who got tired yet never complained because he knew he was doing it for his family. How was it easy for him?

Maybe love is blind, like the one I felt for him. I was still waiting for him, even though he had left me for another woman. Why did I want him to return? To have him next to me, to grow old together, or to make sure that the children did not live with a great emptiness like the absence of a parent?

One day, Eva, who had grown-up then, and talked to me as a friend, asked me: "Mom, if Dad came back one day, would you open the door for him?"

I was tempted to tell her that the door to Anton was always open. Then she asked, "Did you forgive him even if he left you for another woman?"

I was silent for a while. She stared at me with her big black eyes, eyes that were so full of mystery.

"A woman's heart, my daughter, is as big as a sea of suffering, anger, and tears. But the waves of love are powerful; they erase and drown them in the depth, and what remains afterward are forgiveness, kindness, and peace."

BETRAYED

My son, beneath his rude and arrogant behavior, hides a tormented and frightened soul. After my husband left, he fell into a silence that I could not understand. He never asked me about his father, as if he wanted to erase him from his memory, because that was the only way for him not to suffer.

He was an intelligent child. He did very well at school, but from that moment on, he began to change. He didn't study. He didn't even want to go to school. Every time I criticized him, he got tense and raised his voice at me. When he was still young, Eva protected him from the other children, and when he grew up, he was the one to protect her. Who knows if he meant to demonstrate to others that this family had a man and that no one was supposed to mention otherwise.

He attended a cooking class; he cooked at home, and we encouraged him, even when we didn't like the food he prepared. Things then took a bad turn. He argued with friends, got drunk, couldn't find a job that would last him at least a year, and the brother-sister relationship turned into a difficult and challenging one.

One day, Eva told me she needed to talk to me. She looked flustered and confused. She confided to me her usual concern; that is, she felt anxious in these conditions and, if Fabio was going to be released from prison, her life would be in danger.

"Ok, tell me what troubles you, my daughter?"

"Uhm, how could I tell you in a few words? I will be leaving for Milan soon with a group organized by a travel agency."

"Very well! You need to go on a trip. You have locked yourself inside the house. You're much worse than me."

But Eva lowered her head and said something under her breath.

"Sorry, I didn't hear you."

"Mom, I don't intend to come back."

Her voice was low, as if she was afraid that the walls would hear her and collapse from the shock.

"Wait a minute, what are you saying?"

Instinctively, I put my hand on my heart, as if I feared it would stop beating.

"My child, try to be happy here."

But my words sounded strange, unconvincing, and detached from reality, which we both knew well.

"That's not possible. Everywhere I go, I am followed by the shadow of Fabio or of his friends."

"But you have no friends or family in Milan."

"I have a high school friend named Anna. She is married and promised to help me with the documents."

My family was getting smaller; they were escaping, as if they wanted to prove that human beings have in their blood the inclination to seek happiness far away from their family.

After Eva left, Alex felt betrayed. I didn’t know that in a few years we would also leave, in the hope of a better life, but above all, to keep the image of our family alive.

UNDER THE WHITE VEIL (ELENA)

I was happy when my daughter Eva married Diego. She was as beautiful as a flower. Under the white veil, her face radiated joy, but there was sadness too. My heart ached that her father couldn't take her to the altar, but I tried to dispel this thought because I did not want to get sad on that special day.

We hadn't received any letters or phone calls from Anton. Had we made his life so difficult that he didn't remember us even once? Wasn't he curious to see his grown-up children, to know if they looked like him, and, above all, if they had fulfilled their dreams? Did he have another family? Did this family give him fewer problems than we did?

"Where are you?" I asked in a whisper. I thought he would suddenly appear among hundreds of guests to make this day even more memorable, but then I laughed at this ridiculous idea.

Months went by and I wished my daughter would give me a grandchild sooner or later. It was the most beautiful thing I had ever thought of in a long while.

When I watched grandparents walk hand in hand with their grandchildren, I smiled to myself. The youth and vivacity of the grandchildren gave the grandparents a strong desire to live longer.

I waited in vain.

Eva stated that she had no maternal instinct, that she and her husband did not want children, that this was normal in Italy, and that they planned to spend their lives traveling around the world.

"What is the sense of living without children?"

"Oh, mom, I don't want to be like you, who has never been happy."

But I knew well that in her heart she hid a secret that she had shared only with me, and that had certainly influenced her to make this decision.

I slowly gave up and no longer insisted. A woman must surely yearn, dream, and love her child from the first moment she feels it inside her, and onwards, for a lifetime.

I tried to remain friends with her, but living with Alex complicated our relationship.

"Your son is spending your retirement money," she said to me. So, I changed the subject, saying something about the weather forecast, that the day was hot or cold, depending on the season.

I hope that one day we will be like before, laughing, making fun of each other and living our lives in a green meadow where you can plant only peace, a place with no troubles, a place where you can relax under the rays of the sun with a smile on your face. I would have preserved that memory with a camera, and I would never get tired of looking at that picture.

SUAL YET MAGICAL

I've always thought that Diego was a rock where I could rest my head in difficult times. But sometimes I doubt it, especially when I see that he tends to avoid problems. When I tell him about someone who is very sick or that something unpleasant has happened to him, he immediately says something else that had nothing to do with the subject. Or is it simply because he can't concentrate for more than a few minutes?

Yesterday we were watching the news when suddenly we saw our city's cemetery. Dozens of military tanks were transporting the dead who had not won the battle with the virus. I was crying, whereas he grabbed the remote control and changed the channel. Then he apologized, telling me that those scenes were too intense for him to watch.

I stepped onto the balcony. I needed fresh air. I began to watch the garden on the ground floor. The family that lives there has a blond boy of about five. They are the only ones who greet us. The others seem to have vision or hearing problems.

For some reason, during this time, I dream of having a garden in front of the house and planting flowers there. I think of its layout as if Diego and I owned one. In one corner, I would place a bench on which to relax in the spring afternoons and read. On the other side, where the neighbors keep a large dog, I would put ours, which would be a poodle. Of course, that little dog only exists in my mind. I would not remove the tree they have planted in the middle because it would show me the change of seasons. I would see the leaves drop in hundreds and I wouldn't remove them. I love autumn.

At this instant, their son is playing ball. He is alone, but then he calls the dog, which happily played with him. His shouts of joy shattered the silence. I didn't take my eyes off of him. He is wearing a pair of shorts and a blue shirt that match his eye color. He's such a beautiful child!

This view, usual yet magical at the same time, exists even in reality and doesn't just exist on film. Their lives, compared to the boring life that Diego and I live, seem so splendid and wonderful that I inadvertently sigh. A question flashes through my mind: "Would I have wanted a child like him in my life too?"

THE SKY DOESN'T PROMISE ANYTHING GOOD (ELENA)

There is an episode in my daughter's life that I don't want to remember. It made me suffer, but Eva suffered much more; she lost a part of her soul. This event completely changed her life, and I'm convinced that it made her become the woman she is today.

It was a cloudy Sunday. The rain fell on the roof with a steady, regular rhythm.

I tiptoed into Eva's room. I thought that she was sleeping, but then I saw that she had raised the roller shutter and was sitting on the bed.

A gray sky doesn't promise anything good, I thought.

Eva didn't hear me. She was looking at the window, fascinated by the drops of rain sliding down the glass. There was so much sadness in that look! When would sadness leave the threshold of my house?

"Are you awake, sweetheart? I have already prepared breakfast."

She didn't seem to hear me, so I had to ask her again.

"Have breakfast by yourself, Mom. I don't feel like eating."

She wasn't looking at me, but somewhere else beyond the window. She was not in her room, but somewhere far away, in a place where only she and no one else existed.

I took care of the housework, but when she still didn't go out of her room, I went there again, a little bit alarmed. She was there, but this time her gaze was blank, without any expression.

"What's wrong with you? Has anyone threatened you?"

"I'm afraid of making you sad."

"Oh, don't think about that."

"I've been trying to talk to you for a few days, but you have your own problems and I wouldn't want to... "

"I'm your mother, and you are my priority. Talk to me. If I can, I'll help you with all my heart and soul."

Tears began to run down her cheeks, and she couldn't even find the strength to wipe them away. Then, she leaned on my chest, as she did when she was a child, and sighing, she stammered, "I'm pregnant."

Time stopped. The raindrops froze on the glass, resembling tears. My hand remained motionless in her hair for a moment. When the devil comes knocking, you have to open the door.

"Is it Fabio's?"

She nodded.

For the first time, I felt weak, without any ideas or thoughts. I had dreamed of having a grandchild, but not like that. It was a surreal situation, and I couldn't make sense of it. I couldn't find a gentle word to calm her down, much less find a solution.

"Mom, I believed in this love! I invested feelings, sleepless nights, and years, but now I feel like I'm standing on the edge of an abyss. How can I keep this child whose father is in prison?"

"I'm sorry, my daughter. I'd really like to tell you otherwise, but... "

"I can't have it. I don't have to. Not only because my brother would call it a big scandal and would never have accepted it, but because I can't offer anything to this baby."

"We will help you, or rather, I'll help you. Think carefully. You might regret it one day."

"Even you are not convinced about what you are saying, mom. This child would be unfortunate just like me, who grew up without a father. I just want to ask you for something, though."

"What is it, my dear?"

"I want you to be close to me."

"Of course. You shouldn't even ask me that."

"I mean, when I am going to the hospital..."

For the first time, I understood that being a mother was the most difficult job in the world. My mind told me one thing, but my heart said another.

In a voice that I didn't recognize as mine, I whispered, "I'll not leave you alone in a situation like this."

MEMORIES INSIDE THE SUITCASE

When my mother accompanied me to see the gynaecologist at the hospital, I walked, acted, and answered questions like a robot. There were other women waiting in line. I watched as they caressed their bellies with slow hand movements, with a happy smile and dreamy eyes, and I couldn't help but think that I would lose all the things that seemed small and insignificant, but made all the difference. The first visits, the feeling that the baby is moving inside you, the joy of being a mother, that world of emotions that opens up right in front of you---these are all important.

I was determined to do it, but I couldn’t know that the suffering, the doubts, and the guilt were going to be part of me for a long time. When the doctor told me that she was not sure if I would be able to have a child in the future, I felt lost. It seemed to me that her voice came from afar. It was a voice addressed to someone else and not to me.

I was feeling many sensations: they constantly changed and I could not identify them or give them a name. The more I tried to forget or erase this love and its fruit, the more my thoughts tormented me. Even as the days and months passed by, they never left my mind. They were like little clouds on a sunny day; they managed to obscure the light.

While I was preparing my suitcase for my trip to Italy, I took with me a photograph of our family: mom, dad, me and Alex. Alex and I were wrapped up in their embrace. That picture made me laugh because I had my eyes closed. I interpreted this in my own way: I was not sleeping, but simply, I was calm and happy in their presence. I wished that time had remained suspended exactly at that instant, at that moment when we were so happy.

I was hopeful that in another country, a new life and fresh opportunities awaited me. In fact, I still don't regret the decision I made back then.

I thought that the unpleasant memories had drowned beneath the waves of the lake in my city and would no longer disturb me. I could not know that they had secretly occupied a place inside my suitcase.

A NAME, BY MISTAKE

A few days after the wedding ceremony, we left for Paris for our honeymoon. We travelled by the French high-speed train, TGV, which departed from Milan. It was comfortable, and the journey didn't seem long. There was air conditioning, and this gave us the impression that it was also cool outside. It was June, but the weather forecast was unpredictable.

I adored the French capital, and every now and then I thought about how strange life was. I had dreamed of going there with Fabio, but our dream didn't come true and our story ended up like this: uhm, ended... How is it possible that after all the suffering and threats he has given me, I still think about him? Had I loved him so much? Is it true that first love never dies? Or maybe it's because something important tied me to him: a baby who was never born.

He crossed the seas and destroyed my peace of mind. It wasn't fair to think of him in those moments when we were bound for our honeymoon.

We had booked at the four-star hotel "Oceania." The sky was cloudy and threatening, as if a storm would occur at any moment. We hadn't brought an umbrella, but in the hall we were given a large, white one, on which the name of the hotel was written.

On the first day, we stood in line for more than three hours to visit the Eiffel Tower. The staff apologized because, for some technical reasons, only one elevator was working. The weather was constantly changing: sometimes the clouds were thick and covered the top of the tower; sometimes they shifted slightly, allowing the sun to shine brighter than ever; and soon afterwards, the rain fell down. Only the desire to visit the tower did not change.

When we went to the upper floor, I now understood why it was worth the wait: the view was so wonderful that words couldn't even begin to describe it. There were many people; it was impossible to take pictures without the presence of others beside you. We bought a glass of champagne on the last floor.

"Let's have a toast because we finally managed to visit the Eiffel Tower," I said, laughing.

"The toast will be for the two of us and for more fantastic days like this."

We hugged and kissed. There was no past, no suffering, no abandonment in that moment, just me, Diego, and happiness.

In the evening, we went to the swimming pool, which, due to light effects, had taken on a distinct blue color. There were only the two of us in the pool. The proximity to Diego made me feel emotional like the first day of our acquaintance; I clung to him, caressed his hair, alternating between swimming away and towards each other.

Everything would have been beautiful and magical if...

That night, while we were in each other's arms, I, lost in the waves of passion, inadvertently said the name of Fabio. Diego detached himself from me as if he had touched live coal. In that instant, I didn't think much, because I was still immersed in the mystery of another world, a world where our sensations were transformed into whispers, sighs, and incessant declarations of love. I opened my eyes and found myself staring at my angry husband.

"What happened?"

"You said Fabio," he reprimanded me.

I felt my heart grow heavy. Why are joys doomed to perish so quickly?

"Oh, how was that possible? Forgive me, but there's only you in my life."

My words, although indisputably true, seemed pathetic, weak, and without the power of persuasion.

In the days following that episode, we were sometimes close, other times distant, like the weather that was constantly changing.

I hated myself for ruining the magnificence of a trip I had always dreamed of.

Over the years, when there was no more passion between us, I thought that my husband had never forgotten that name I whispered during our honeymoon. Like me, I also hadn't forgotten that person who, although thousands of kilometres away, had found a way into my life, trying to destroy the present that I had built with so much effort and sacrifice.

ARK AREA (ELENA)

I spoke with my son today over Skype. But what am I saying? I talk to him and Eva several times every day. All that is left to us now are the phone calls.

He told me he felt alone and desperate, and that he blamed himself for leaving Italy.

"But you left in search of a better life. How could you have known such hardship was going to come?"

"I can hardly wait for the day when flights will resume. I miss you, Mom."

He seemed like a child who always needed me, who took two steps and turned to me for approval, who wrote his ABCs in the notebook upon my encouragement, who fell to the ground and needed just a kiss from me to stop the pain.

I tell him that these days I feel tired, that here in Bergamo there is an atmosphere of fear, and that I hope that this situation will end as soon as possible.

"Have you talked to anyone on the phone?" he asks me. I mention about talking with my sisters and relatives from Albania, but he seems distracted. Perhaps he wants to know how Eva is, but he never asks about her directly. I tell him that she is fine, although to me she seems a bit nervous and pensive.

Alex doesn't say anything. Maybe he'd like to talk to her too. It is useless to ask him, though, because he is never open about his feelings. He didn't even say anything when his father left.

Once, I asked him: "Do you miss your father?"

Without looking into my eyes, he answered: "Even when he was with us, he was always far away. I have lived many more years without him than with him. No, I don't miss him."

"But you surely must think of him sometimes," I wanted to add, but I remained silent.

One day, I found him leafing through a family album. He stared at the photos for a long time, as if trying to bring up the past or if he was just nostalgic. I was then convinced that he did have some feelings.

The fact that he was arrogant with Eva didn't mean that he didn't love her. I thought he was just trying to disguise his fragile, difficult and contradictory character, of which he was a victim. However, there is a dark area in his life that ultimately separated him from his sister.

FISH IN THE AQUARIUM

I was at home with Alex when I heard moans coming from his room. For a moment, I thought the sound was coming from the TV, but after a while, I realized it wasn't that. It was his voice, complaining. Apparently, he wasn't feeling well.

I opened the door and found him lying on the bed with his half-shut eyes.

"Alex, my son, what's happened?"

I panicked, because we're in a foreign country. I can barely pronounce a few words in Italian under normal circumstances, let alone when I'm worried sick.

I called Eva and told her to come right away. I wandered around the house and was uneasy. I went back to his room, but he was in a strange state. He was breathing heavily, speaking, moaning, and crying at the same time. He would have a fever, I thought.

I took a small, damp towel and put it on his forehead.

When Eva arrived, I bombarded her with instructions; I told her to call for first aid immediately because her brother was very sick.

She entered the room, cold and unsympathetic as she was, as if she were a doctor and had everything under control. Alex looked calmer, but he was pale and his lips were dry.

"I'm going to get him a glass of water," I stammered. I was in a hurry, but Eva grabbed me by the arm.

"What's wrong?"

"Can't you see? Your son is high on drugs."

She had a habit of exaggerating.

"Don't talk nonsense!"

Eva pointed to the bedside table, and there in the middle, I saw something that caught my attention: a syringe on top of a white piece of paper.

I was shocked. I didn't want to believe what I was seeing, and the first thought that came to my mind was that someone else had left it there. But who, when it was just the two of us at home?

I sat down and my son's life passed before my eyes: the way he changed when his father left; his cynical, rude, and aggressive behavior with his sister and me; the constant change of jobs; and his total dependence on me. Apparently, he was also dependent on other things.

How did I not see it before? Was I that blind? Or was this his first time on drugs? When did this happen? I got a hold of my thoughts as this was not a time for endless analysis.

I got up and said to Eva in a commanding voice, "Thank you for opening my eyes! Now call for first aid immediately!"

We were so close to each other like we had never been before.

My daughter didn't move. She gave the impression that she was there by mistake. She was silent for a moment, and then, without batting an eyelash, she said, "Mommy, don't be alarmed at all. He will get better. You'll see, nothing will happen to him".

She then went away, leaving me alone with my son, and now no one knew what direction his life would take.

It seemed to me that I was a fish that longed for the sea, but fate was cruel and had thrown it into the confined space of an aquarium, constantly beating itself against the glass, seeking freedom and salvation.

REAMS THAT VANISH

Anything could have happened to my son that day, and I felt completely desolate and helpless beside him. Luckily, he was then breathing normally, his face lost its pale color, and he opened his eyes and smiled at me.

His hair was cut short, and the tuft fell over his forehead. His dark eyes and his lips turning a rosy shade of pink told me he was back to normal.

I would have given everything to see him happy, or at least lead a normal life, but then it's not up to me.

"Mom, I'm hungry."

I took his hands in mine, caressed them as if he were a child, and asked: "Sweetheart, *why*?"

He shook his head as if to tell me, "You don't understand."

I got up to make him a sandwich, and my thoughts were racing through my head, trying to find the right words to say.

I thought you were strong, Alex. For me, you are the one who maintains the balance in this family, but now I know you well: you are so weak! I came here to retire peacefully, to help you and to be close to you during difficult times, but your entire life is made up solely of these instants.

I wanted to see you settled with a job, independent and with your own family. My dreams of you are shattered, like the dreams in the night that vanish the next morning.

I don't know where I went wrong. Was it because I alone fought in this battle? Would your path have been the same if I had my husband, your father, next to me?

Open your heart to mom, my son! I have never known your thoughts and feelings because you have locked them in a safe, and only you have the key.

A SNOWFLAKE (ALEX)

When Dad abandoned us, what I felt was not a void, but a desire to grow up quickly and become the man of the house. My classmates made fun of me, saying that I didn't have a father. I couldn't forget their scornful laughter until, one day, something changed within me: I couldn't stand them anymore, so I punched all of them.

I saw Eva grow up and become more beautiful, and I felt the need to protect her. When my friends at the bar told me that my sister had a mobster for a boyfriend, I lost my cool and I was transformed into another person, someone that even I didn't recognize.

When my sister went to Italy, I felt bad. After dad, another important person in my life was leaving. At the disco one Saturday, someone gave me drugs, and I just couldn't resist it. It soon developed into a habit. I had hoped that it would help me become carefree and indifferent. I was for a while, but the effects didn't last long. When its effect ended, I felt emptier and more depressed than ever.

I started walking into a dead end, which would expose my weaknesses and insecurities. I wasn't able to find a job and a long-term relationship. I thought it was the fault of the city where I lived, Albania. I went to Italy to escape from myself and from my vices, but above all, to be close to Eva and to re-establish my ties with my sister. I dreamed of a quiet life, but I couldn't get rid of the demons inside me.

Things did not go as planned. I felt alone because I only had you, Mom, because my sister was drifting further away from me. I couldn't find a way to make peace with her. Maybe a "sorry" would have been enough. But it was so hard to say, so much effort to admit that I was wrong! I know that my dad would never have wanted to see me like this. However, I swear to you, Mom, that this will be the first and last time. My promise won't be like a snowflake that melts as soon as it hits the ground.

TROUBLED SOULS

It is Sunday, and the sky is blue, but its beauty has no effect on me. The silence is intense, and so is the pain. Life has lost its value; it has been transformed into numbers, which are increasing at a dizzying speed. But they are not just numbers; they are lives, experiences, love stories and precious memories.

When Diego comes back from shopping, he seems absent-minded. He's sweating profusely. He is still wearing a mask and a pair of gloves, but from the quick blinking of his eyes, I guess that he is agitated.

"What's up? You look strange. "

"It is so weird out there. People are afraid, and they act cold and robotic. Today, a quarrel ensued at the supermarket because someone asked the other person to wear a mask properly. They almost punched each other. Who would have thought that people would argue over a mask?"

I helped him put things in order. He has also bought a bottle of Pinot Grigio, a white wine.

"And this?"

"Did you forget? Tomorrow is my birthday."

"Oh, forgive me," I say, embarrassed by my forgetfulness.

Every day seems the same nowadays, even if the dates try to remind us of something important in our lives.

I feel a bit sad. No gifts for Diego, no dinner in a restaurant with relatives and friends, no trips.

"We had made lots of plans for today," I mumbled.

"It is important to be in good health. After that, we can take all the trips we want."

What he just said sounds like music to my ears. It gives me reassurance that we will still be together in the future.

Diego doesn't talk much, doesn't make promises, and doesn't give compliments, but when he says something, it is always true.

In these trying times, the two of us are bound by an invisible thread, which may seem thin, but which brings our troubled souls closer than ever before. We talk about the journeys we have taken over the years, the adventures, the jokes, and the laughter. It's a way of admitting that we have had a great time together and have felt good in each other's presence.

IECES OF PAPER AND GREETINGS

Those pieces of paper are still at home. Memories are often more real than reality itself. Years ago, I went to my country of origin for a week, and the day I returned to Italy was my birthday. Diego had suggested that we go to a restaurant that evening, but I had refused. I would certainly be tired from the trip, and I would prefer not to go out.

Walking along the paths or by the lakeside, I was accompanied in every step by memories, the images of a tormented past. Those memories made me feel apprehensive. It seemed to me that Fabio would appear at any moment and everything would go wrong. I don't know what I was going to say to him if he were in front of me. The only thing I felt during those moments was *fear*.

I thought of my father and his sense of humor, his sincerity, his magnificence, and his strength, but with the passing of years, the memories started to fade away. I clung to some significant chapters in our lives and tried to give those colors and shades, because this was the only way to remember them. I didn't want to ever forget my dad.

Trips to my homeland were also rare because we now lived in Italy. But I needed them because I felt like I was going there to relive my life story. I saw it as a tree with roots deep into the earth; I watered and took care of it. When I was among those who spoke my mother tongue, I felt free from my feelings of inferiority brought about by living in a foreign land.

Upon my return, I recalled those precious moments with relatives and friends, the bonds between us broken because of the distance.

Diego waited for me at *Orio al Serio* airport. I missed him and our phone calls were not enough for me. I also missed our apartment, the smell of the furniture, the messy study room, the computer, which peeked out from beneath notebooks and books, and Diego's multi-colored sweatshirts dangling haphazardly from hangers.

As I entered the house, a large vase of red carnations placed at the center of the table caught my eye. I put the suitcase on the floor and embraced him.

"You are the most romantic man I've ever known!" I said to him, and we both started to laugh out loud. My husband has never been a romantic man until today.

As I went around the house, I found pieces of paper here and there on which he wrote "Happy Birthday"; inside the shower cubicle, in the wardrobe, in the drawer, on the computer keyboard.

When we sat down at the table, I was filled with joy. He had bought two boxes of pizza and had placed beers in the fridge. I talked nonstop. I told him about my trip and that it would have been better if he was there with me. I didn't even admit to myself that being close to him made my fears and the shadows of the past disappear.

Every time I read those notes, I feel nostalgic--for what we were and perhaps for what we can be in the future.

We live in an ivory tower, isolated from the pain that has attacked humanity. With a glass of beer in hand, we give salute to an uncertain future, a future that is as wavering as the flame of the candle that we've put in the middle of the table.

Happy birthday and many more to come, but not like this please….

EATH LOOKS AT NO ONE IN THE FACE (ELENA)

I think I have been infected with the damn virus. I have only met a few people, but the usual bar I went to was so big that it could accommodate the entire city's population; the tables were so close to one another that you could hear each other's conversations. I could have been infected there. I hope not. Honestly, I'm not afraid of death. It will happen only for an instant, just like falling asleep and not remembering anything. I'm only sad because I will not see my children again. I will miss them.

But what am I saying? With death, I'll no longer have feelings; I'll no longer feel cold or hot. I will not be hungry anymore, I will lose desire and affection, and I will become unemotional.

I would like to live a bit longer to see my son with a woman by his side and build a family; I would like to see them together, brother and sister, as they were during their childhood. After these things happen, I'm ready to leave this world.

Alex was calm on the phone. He had found a psychologist online and felt relieved when he told her his concerns. I miss him so much because we were used to each other and we shared a life together, with all the good and bad things that go with it.

He seems more mature and more responsible now. This period of isolation helped us reflect on life and understand things that, due to our hectic life, we hadn't realized before. Realization will come to him, for he doesn't lack intelligence.

I would have liked to grow old with my husband, spending winter afternoons together while sipping hot coffee or tea. I would also love to walk during summer nights in the park, accompanied by a grandchild. Eva would tell me that I'm obsessed, that I always think of the same things, and that I should enjoy and love what I have right now. She said that no one lives the life that they want to have; we all try and fight for it, but we are powerless against destiny.

Who said that I don't like my life? Except during this time, of course. When I open my eyes in the morning and see the sky, blue or cloudy, I love the day all the same. But I also like to dream.

I haven't heard anything about Anton for a long time. I got news about him every now and then, but those stories were sometimes exaggerated. Oftentimes they arrived in fragments, and were being pieced together, creating half-truth information. Some said he was in Greece, others said Tirana or Pogradec, and that he had a new family.

Only God knows if he has achieved the life he dreamed of. I would have liked to meet him, even just once. I would have stared at his wrinkled face and lean body, staggering with slow steps and maybe with a cane in his hand, with his hair as white as snow. When we were young, we often joked about us growing old, which seemed so distant and far away.

How was life treating him? Has he found the peace he was looking for? Has he ever felt remorse for leaving us?

If he was standing in front of me, I would ask him if he loved me or if he ever loved us. If it were so, how could he abandon us? Has he been looking for us all these years? Has he ever thought of the old stove, where the four of us warmed our hands, of the empty refrigerator, or of the cheerful laughter of our children when he came home and didn't just bring presents, but the whole world itself?

With nostalgia, I remember those details that made us happy, because happiness is made up of different moments.

On television, it is said that the *elderly* are the most at risk. It just seems natural that they are the ones at risk, maybe because the pain of this loss does not seem so excruciating. Don't say this word too often. Do you know why? Because in the blink of an eye, you will find yourself becoming old too.

Many people lose their lives every day! I have never felt such despair! Tears roll down my cheeks as soon as I hear sad stories. Eva told me that two of Diego's friends lost their battle with the virus. They were my son-in-law's age, 45 years old. Isn't it terrible? Death looks at no one in the face. It does not discriminate.

One afternoon, the ambulance came and took our neighbour to the hospital. I watched the scene from the window. My soul was shattered. She is younger than me. They laid her on the stretcher and someone put the oxygen cylinder on her. She lives alone and has no children. Her dog followed her into the courtyard, then began to bark and howl with a kind of pain that no human could express.

I believe in love and all its variations. Only love can help us overcome the difficult state we are in right now.

FORGOTTEN SENSATIONS

A car from civil protection goes around the city and encourages people not to go out of their homes. Then there is absolute silence. The buses are all empty. Who knows what the drivers think and feel while driving around a ghost town?

Diego has bought the *L'eco di Bergamo* newspaper from a nearby kiosk.

"Give it to me after you read it," I tell him.

When I get a hold of it, each letter weighs like a ton. I read the headline: *In March, the city of Bergamo had 4,500 deaths, excluding those who had died in their apartments or in nursing homes, so the figure is double that of the official one.*

I closed the newspaper. I can read no further. I watch over the window, beyond it. When will we get out of this nightmare?

"Eva, will you come out onto the balcony?"

I nod in agreement. I need to breathe fresh air.

Diego has built a wooden bench there. I never thought of sitting on it before. But now it is different: I am eager to try new things to take my mind off this situation.

We sit side by side, as if we were in a park. We watch the trees that quiver in the light breeze and the red roses in the gardens that are losing their petals. It's as if they're so close that you can touch them if you merely reach out to them.

The sun is gradually setting and, every now and then, a cloud hides its transition. The shadows flicker like the light inside a room.

"One second," Diego says, going inside the house. I turn west and let my hair be caressed by the wind.

A short time has passed since I last saw my mother, but it seems like so long ago; we used to invite her often, and Diego was happy to cook for her. We smiled when she spoke in Italian and, without missing a beat, she substituted the words she didn't know with Albanian ones. Thus, a mix of languages.

Her arrival added notes of joy to our existence. Who knows why our mundane life has turned us into robots, depriving us of some of the most beautiful sensations? Our hectic life, which followed exactly the same pattern, drowned most of our emotions.

Diego reappears with two glasses of wine.

"I'm drunk without putting the alcohol on my lips."

My husband surprises me these days. He is attentive to the little things that I once thought he was not even aware of. This situation had to arrive in order to bring out his romantic side, which he had kept hidden as if at the bottom of a well.

We toast our glasses and stare into each other's eyes. We haven't done this simple act in a long while. Our eyes are always fixed on our cell phone screens, liking, commenting, and congratulating each other. Sometimes we even feel envious of others. Let's not forget to mention the large television screen.

The horizon appears to be a backdrop displaying a million colors. Diego takes my hand as if it were our first date. We kiss each other passionately. Our lips taste like wine as we kiss. The kiss evokes a thousand forgotten sensations. My heart is beating fast. It hasn't been like this for a long time, as if I did not exist before.

The sun is now used to us being out there, and it no longer spies on us. It sinks beneath the horizon, and the sky takes on a deep orange tint. Diego hugs me and whispers, "Let's go to the bedroom."

I don't want to close my eyes. I look at him as he kisses me, whispering sweet words of love, with his curls slightly damp with sweat; he breathes fast and he moves rhythmically, awakening in me a world of feelings and emotions that I haven't experienced for a long time. I slowly closed my eyes and let him guide my soul on a journey where there is only passion, love, peace, and infinite freedom.

THE SAFEST REFUGE

Mom doesn't answer my morning call, so I keep on calling her number.

Can't she hear the phone ring? Has something happened? Does she feel sick? Thousands of questions, with no answers forthcoming.

Hours pass by before she calls me. I feel my spirit lift up, becoming worry-free.

"Mom, you freaked me out. Where were you?"

"I don't remember anything, my daughter, maybe I fainted. I was lying down, and now that I feel OK, I immediately called you."

Something breaks inside of me. It is the certainty that my family and I are in good health, despite the fact that death is all around us, taking lives one by one.

"Have you got a fever?"

"No, I don't think so."

She sounds strange. I want to reassure her, but I find it hard to do so since I'm in a state of complete panic.

"Did you eat something?"

"Yes, a small amount of soup."

"A small amount of soup?"

"Even that was difficult to swallow."

I try to keep the tears and worry at bay.

"Don't worry, mom, you're just tired."

But I'm not sure. We have been locked up at home, and it's unusual to be tired, except mentally.

"I hope so."

"Listen, mom. Diego will go shopping, and I'll tell him to bring you some ready-made food, so you don't need to cook. Ah, how I wish to be close to you!"

"Me too."

"Do you need anything?"

"Oh, nothing. I have no appetite at all."

Another alarm bell goes off inside of me.

"Rest now, I'll call you later."

I hang up the phone, and I can't stop myself from crying.

"Why are you crying?" Diego asks me.

"I'm concerned about Mom. I think she has the coronavirus. Where could she have gotten it?

From a bar, from a neighbor, from me? But then, we haven't seen each other for a while."

"Think positive!"

How did my husband come up with this expression?

"It's easy for you to say. She is my mom."

"It's too early to be alarmed."

Diego comes closer to me. For me, his embrace is the safest refuge; from there, the world appears to be better and free of problems.

The clock is ticking loudly, as if to heighten my fear of a tomorrow that has become a mystery.

PLEASE SAVE THIS WOMAN!

The telephone calls with my mother have become increasingly intense. Her temperature rises in the afternoon. I talk to the doctor, who advises that she begins antibiotic treatment right away. He cannot visit her at home due to the high risk of infection.

Mom is stuttering and dragging her words out. I can hardly recognize her. She is a strong woman who never got sick or stayed long in bed.

How did we end up in this predicament? I want to scream, to let out the rage that has been building up for weeks. Why did this happen to her? Why not me? I still need her. Not to mention my brother, who, if he finds out, will go out of his mind.

A few days passed, but the antibiotics didn't work at all. When her temperature drops, I'm full of hope and faith that things will get better. If not, I will fall back into the abyss of fear and sadness.

I dialed 112 one afternoon. I explained my mother's situation, but the voice on the other end of the line is cold and distant, as if it came from another continent.

"We can't admit her to the hospital if she doesn't have any breathing problems or a low oxygen level in her blood."

"She is alone at home with no one to look after her."

"That is not a valid reason. The hospitals are overflowing."

They hang up the phone to answer someone else's call, probably saying the standard lines.

I feel trapped: four walls surround me everywhere I turn. Even if she can't speak, I beg my mother to return my calls. I'd like to know how she's doing. Without saying anything, she nods her head in agreement.

My mother's fever continues to rise, and after a few days, she begins to have breathing problems.

When I explain the situation to first responders, they ask for my mother's address and other personal information. They promise that they will be there as soon as possible.

In silence, Diego and I get ready. He's no longer able to calm me down. He, too, is worried.

We have no idea what to think because everything happens in the blink of an eye. We get in the car, wearing the masks that have now become a part of our faces and lives.

When the ambulance arrives with the alarm siren on, we're down in the courtyard of her building. This time, the siren isn't for a stranger; it's for someone I know, someone who is a part of my family, a person who is a part of my soul.

I used my duplicate keys to open the door, but I wasn't able to get in. I imagined myself using these keys ten or twenty years from now, when my mother would be very old and unable to leave her bed.

With a heavy heart, I go down the stairs. Someone looks curiously behind the glass. Diego assures me that she will now be under the care of doctors and will improve. He would have reassured me if it had happened at a different time, but I've watched a lot of news and programs, and I know that the situation in the hospitals is tragic; there are no vacancies, and they'll have to wait a long time before they can secure a place.

They put her on a stretcher and took her away. This is the woman who gave me life, raised me alone while making many sacrifices, loved me even when I made mistakes, and respected my every decision, even if she didn't like them.

"Please save this woman!" I cried out loud.

"We will do everything possible," someone says quietly, as if to persuade himself first.

My mother tries to smile as she opens her eyes.

"Mommy, stay calm," I tell her in our native tongue, which no one understands in this city where even the air is foreign.

They won't even let me get close enough to kiss her.

I cheered her up by joining my hands in the shape of a heart to express my undying love for her.

"Don't worry, sweetheart; I'll be right back!"

This is Elena, my mother, who gives me strength in the most trying times of her life.

The ambulance departs. Because my eyes are filled with tears, I can't see the path it takes.

THE GAME OF RAINDROPS

The bedroom is dark, with only a sliver of light filtering in through the shutters. It is much like my hope, which is now very faint. I pick up the phone but toss it back on the bedside table, wishing it would not ring. Diego is acutely aware of my every move.

"Try to stay calm," he says quietly, as if he's afraid of scaring the night.

But how can I be calm? I toss and turn in bed, unable to find comfort, until he gets up and goes to the other room.

He doesn't even have to work the next day. What would have happened to him tonight if he had stayed close to me?

Because I'm anxious, the bed is no longer a safe haven for me. I imagine myself getting up and rushing to the hospital, which has been inaccessible for a long time. It would only take a split second for me to see my mother. Tell her she has me, that I love her, and that she must do everything possible not to leave me alone.

How does she feel as she watches the nurses come and go while she has a desperate need for oxygen and tries to win over death? Scared or lost? My heart aches for her.

Mom, please don't leave me! I'd like to take your pain, cough, and breathing problems and put them into my body.

A new day is approaching, and my gloomy thoughts are already exhausted. The sun fills me with optimism and hope. My mother is a strong woman who has no other illnesses and will live to see another day. Also, I'm out here waiting for her. Or does that make no difference at all?

While they were taking her away in the ambulance, I remembered her slightly pale appearance, her hair falling over her shoulders, and her affectionate gaze.

The phone isn't turned off when I call her. I live with the illusion that she is fine and will at any moment answer me. But there's nothing but silence.

I get up and move from one room to the other. My husband suggests that we go for a walk around the building within the distance allowed by law. He claims that if we don't do it, we'll go insane. I shook my head in refusal. It seems too late now, because I think I have just gone crazy. The only place I'd like to spend the night is in the hospital with my mother.

I switched on my computer. On the news, victims who did not survive the difficult battle against the coronavirus can be seen. So many numbers! So many lives! I hope my mom doesn't become one of those numbers.

I step out onto the balcony to gaze at the sky. The sky is cloudy, and the first raindrops are falling. They enlarge like spots as soon as they touch the asphalt, and I get a whiff of wet earth. While the raindrops wet my hair and body and look like tears on my face, I raise my head, perhaps to nothing or to an omnipotent force, and silently pray.

"Please don't leave me, Mom!" I whisper, and the play of raindrops on the asphalt is the only image that my lost self remembers.

INFINITE LONELINESS

There hasn't been any news in a few days. When my phone rings, I am startled. It's from an unlisted phone number. They will definitely help me when speaking with her. Until now, this has been the method of communication between sick patients and their relatives.

"Good morning. Are you Mrs. Elena Gega's daughter? "

"Yes, I am," I answer, confused.

"I'm sorry to inform you that your mother passed away just a few minutes ago."

Time stopped. I had no idea a phrase could pierce your body and heart like a sword and inflict so much suffering.

"No, it's not possible!"

"We stayed close to her until the very end, giving her strength and holding her hand."

I imagine their gloved hands, our absence from her side, and the infinite loneliness that my mother suffered in that hospital bed. The voice continued to say something, but I was no longer paying attention. I hand the phone over to Diego.

I'm exhausted. With rage, I stare up at the sky. I despise the virus that may have been deliberately sent from China to kill my mother and hundreds of others. It feels like a curse that I wasn't kissing, hugging, and telling her how much I loved her.

Who will provide me with a love like hers? Who will accept and love me for who I am? She only looked at the bright side of things, knew how to forgive others, and never judged them.

My husband is sitting next to me on the couch. I realize he has tears in his eyes. He hugs me and softly whispers, "I'm sorry. I loved Elena as if she were my mother." I'm going to miss her terribly!"

We continued to hug each other. The anguish has taken away the ability to speak, and the stillness is excruciating.

How did she spend her final moments? Was she in pain? Did she think she felt abandoned by us? Or is it more of fate?

Every time we talked about these turbulent times, she told me that she felt sorry for people who left like this, without receiving a caress or a blessing. She has become one of them now.

My husband starts preparing hot tea while I begin crying again.

Everything is surreal. Under normal circumstances, I would have been close to her, we would have welcomed the people who came to offer us their condolences, and we would have accompanied her to her final resting place. Now, the only thing we can do is sip tea and share memories of her.

"She was gone too soon, just in a few days! She deserved to live some better days."

"Elena was happy with you and with us," adds Diego.

"I really hope so."

"Don't doubt about it. Do you remember how much we used to laugh when she came here? And when we went to Riccione, she was beside us during the walks. She took you by the hand and said, "I don't want to bore you, but I'm afraid of getting lost in this chaotic city."

"She seemed frail, but she was a strong woman," I say, more to myself than to him.

"When my mother died after much pain, I felt like an orphan. She protected me from the atrocities of the world. I turned my head and there was nothing but emptiness around me. There was no longer her who followed me with a look, who covered me with a blanket on cold winter nights, who gave me advice and told me 'I love you so much', who silently wished me happiness. It was just at that moment that I had to grow up and face reality. But... I would have liked to remain a child in her arms," Diego said.

Diego's words amaze me. He had never told me about these sentiments.

"I'm sorry I was not able to tell her how important she was in my life."

"Eva, she knew that, she understood it. Don't be sad. Ah, tomorrow we have to get Elena's things."

"I can't make it."

"I know how difficult it is for you. I will go by myself. It is not at all easy for me either."

The sun makes its usual path towards the west. It will be the first night without Mom.

THE PERSONAL EFFECTS

I'm still in bed when Diego goes to retrieve my mother's personal effects. God knows how much I miss her! I called her every morning and afternoon. She was my mother and my friend. We often argued, but after a second, we forgot all about it and joked like nothing had happened.

I see my days as empty and colorless. The sense of guilt does not leave me. What if I stayed at her house? At least we would have been together. Or would nothing have changed the path of this tragic fate?

My husband enters the house, and his face looks emaciated and suffering. He holds a black bag, which he doesn't know where to put. He hesitates a bit, then he places it on the chair.

I got up immediately. I am shocked and excited. I ask Diego if they have told him anything in particular, and he replies, annoyed, "The same things they repeat to others in the same situation, so only when we get out of this lockdown can we have her funeral."

With trembling hands, I open the bag: I find folded blouses, pajamas, underwear, glasses, a cell phone, and a bottle of water.

I smell the clothes and inhale mom's scent, fresh like a rose. I put my head over them and tears flowed down my cheeks. Diego approaches and caresses my hair. He tells me not to cry because we will never forget Elena, and that she would never have wanted to see me suffer.

I go to the bedroom and, in the wardrobe, I move my clothes. I find a space for my mother's clothes. I imagine her putting them on, and my heart cries when I think that this vision will never become a reality.

I sit exhausted on the sofa and turn on her cell phone. Missed calls attract my attention on its screen. They are mine. I check if my mom tried to call me, but there is not any calls. I look at the sent messages. I open my eyes wide, as if I had vision problems. There are three messages there: two that she has sent to Alex and one to me, but surprisingly I haven't received it.

THE WAY A BROTHER IS LOVED

It is my mother's last memory. I try to imagine her in the moments when she has written it. Surely, she must have realized that she had only a few hours left and that those lines were the only thread that connected her to me.

I hardly dare breathe. It seems unfair that I couldn't be close to her to ease her pain, that I couldn't hold her hand in mine as she had done during all of my difficult times, and that I couldn't say "goodbye" to her. Even the most dreadful scenario could not have foreseen this.

I'm not sure why I'm afraid to read it. It's as if after reading it, my anguish will be deeper and more painful than her death. Finally, I decide to read it again and again in order to decipher the message hidden behind those words: "Sweetheart, this virus is killing me. But don't despair for me. I just wanted to say that you and Alex were the best gifts I've ever received in life. Please love each other. A big hug from me."

I held the cell phone in my hand, this silent and lifeless object that was trying to convey to me my mom's love. She had touched it for the last time. Because of that, I can feel her close to me.

I shouldn't be reading the texts she's written to Alex, but my curiosity won't let go of me. I'd like to know more about her feelings in those final moments, which were slipping away like grains of sand from her fingers.

I'm not sure if Alex has been informed that Mom has passed away. It must be agonizing for him, being so far away. Even those of us who were only a few steps away from her couldn't do anything for her.

My son, I am writing to you from the hospital. Anyway, I have lived my life. I hope someday you will be happy because you deserve it. You are the sweetest and most sensitive person I have ever known. Ah, Eva asks me constantly about you; she loves you just the way a brother is loved.

I don't understand this message. It seems to me that it hasn't been written by Mom but by someone else. *Eva asks me constantly about you.* That isn't true. I never asked her about Alex. On the contrary, I got nervous when she mentioned his name.

Then everything became clear to me. My mother always hoped that I had a good relationship with my brother; she hoped that sooner or later, the storm would subside and peace would come between us. Until the end, she tried to bring us both closer. Perhaps that was her biggest dream.

THE BENCHES OF THE TRAIN STATION

Some fragments of the past did not leave me; they stayed with me and kept me company; that difficult night when Alex was battling his demons, my preoccupied mom, and my leaving them.

According to her, I had been selfish, cold, and indifferent when I left Alex in that state. She couldn't know how much that situation made me suffer.

My brother and I were not close, but when I saw that he had entered a dead end, where darkness prevailed, it seemed to me that this was happening to me personally. My anger and resentment subsided. To me, he seemed so fragile and helpless! But the words I pronounced, for who knows why, were harsh, strong, and hurt like stones, but none of them expressed my true, inner feelings.

I hated Alex, that stubborn and aggressive boy who always tried to keep situations under control. My brother was the child who shielded me from others, who sat on the school's stairs waiting for me so we could go home together, who sat on the sofa with me and watched my favorite movies, and who helped me with Math.

Not the one who was drugged up in bed.

That evening, the distance between us seemed insurmountable, and I no longer hoped to find common ground with him. But deep inside, I prayed that Alex would recover and that I would never see him like that again. I had conflicting feelings that I couldn't handle at that time.

I pushed him away from me, not to be calm or happy myself, but to encourage him to analyse his mistakes and reflect on them. The more I avoided him, the more he entered my thoughts.

When I saw that Mom was a little bit nervous, I sensed the reason. When I told her that she didn't have to give Alex money so that he will look for a job, she objected. "Eva, can't you see? He is my son, part of my soul. If I don't help him, if I'm not close to him, he'll end up on the streets, on the benches of the train station.

"That's where he belongs!" I angrily answered.

For me, the best solution was for her to close the door and drive him away. How could I know that a mother would never abandon her child?

Every time I passed by the station, my gaze stopped on the benches. I watched the people who, at sunset, lied on them, covered with old blankets, abandoned by fate, without a job or a home. I imagined my brother there for a split second, but then I erased that thought because I felt bad.

Mom's second message is short, as if she felt that she had a limited amount of time at her disposal. *Alex, I'm sorry that I won't see you and Eva happy together, just like when you were children. I miss you...*

VICTIMS OF FATE

I can't stay away from the cell phone. My heart feels heavy with pain and nostalgia. I have read many testimonies of people who have lost a parent or two during this period.

I have lost my mom now and, years ago, my father.

During that time, there hasn't been a single day when I didn't think of him. But when he started missing my birthdays, holidays, or other important events, I didn't think about him anymore. A message from him would have made me happy, but it never arrived. I understood that it would be better to put the memory of him in a corner of my mind.

When I talked to Mom, it seemed as if Dad did not belong in the past; he was still a part of her life; he was just working far away, and we would see him soon.

One day, I asked her: "Mommy, how do you feel about Dad? Do you hate him?"

She paused for a while.

"No, my soul, I can't. He is your father and the only man who taught me what love is. I'll always be grateful to him that he has left me a great treasure. You, my children."

I stared at her in disbelief.

"Alex and I have given you a lot of problems."

"Eh, my daughter, you are my life."

Where did she get her strength and all that affection?

One day, she came to pay us a visit after lunch. Diego went out to leave us alone. Her gray hairs are visible under the sunlight.

"Why don't you dye them? They have turned white as snow."

"I don't want to hide anything, sweetheart. Those gray hairs are the years that I have lived, and I'm proud of them."

"Tell me the truth. Would you like to see Papa?"

"He now has his family. It wouldn't be fair. But maybe yes, I would like to meet him even just once."

"And what would you tell him? That he turned out to be a coward for abandoning us when we needed him?"

Her face became pensive.

"I'm sad that you ran away because you lost the gift of being the parent of two wonderful children and the husband of a woman who will love you for the rest of her life."

"With all the troubles that Alex brings to you?" I insisted.

"He has changed. He no longer gives in to the vices and addictions of the past. But you know, my sweetheart, life often leaves us with no choice and we are only victims of fate or circumstances."

SO WE LOST THE FEELING

It's been a month since we are locked up in the house. Time goes by even when you cannot go out and enjoy the daylight, when you suffer or are sad, or when you don't live life as it should be lived.

I didn't close my eyes last night. The bed knew my anguish. I got up trying not to make any noise so as not to wake Diego. I turned on the computer and started looking at the photos, the old ones, black and white, that I've scanned. In all of them, my mother emitted radiance, even if the road she followed was unpaved, full of holes and obstacles.

"Mom, you deserved to be happy. You should not have left so soon," I thought.

"But I'm happy," she had told me once. "I am healthy, I've my children and my sisters. What more could I want?"

"A man by your side," I wanted to add, but I remained silent.

I thought that you could find happiness only if you had someone by your side, otherwise you would feel lost, incomplete. This thought, surely, must have stemmed from my insecurities.

But my mom was a strong woman; she never complained and didn't try to get to know anyone after dad left.

I stare at the photo in which she, sitting between me and Alex, wrapped us in her arms. Her eyes were alight with joy, as if she had the whole world in her hands. For her, this was true happiness.

I hear my husband walking towards the kitchen. A new day has come, without mom. Who knows if I once counted the dawns without Dad beside me?

"Diego, please bring me a glass of warm milk," I holler at him.

"Coming."

He opens the refrigerator, takes the milk, pours it into the glass, heats it in the microwave and heads for the bedroom. He thinks that I'm still lying on the double bed. For how long have we become invisible to each other?

"I'm here in the studio. Didn't you hear me when I got up?"

"I didn't notice," he replies.

It's like as if we are in a hide and seek game. This is how we lost each other, or it would be better to say, this is how we lost the feeling.

He who always came home late, who pursued his own passions which are different from mine. He who watched action films, and I, the romantic ones. He, who didn't listen to some of the things I said, because my phrases were too long and the description too detailed.

Suddenly the doorbell rings. It's the postman. My husband goes out and comes back with a big package in his hands.

THE SURPRISE

Diego's face is indecipherable as if he has no idea what's inside the package. He places it on the table and doesn't touch it.

"It's for you!" he tells me, and he has a mischievous smile on his face.

Ah, it means that he knows what's inside!

I don't waste a minute and I start to open it. I become clumsier as I am getting more excited to unveil it, thus prolonging the moment of surprise.

"What is that?"

He doesn't answer.

I finally see it: it's an album. I start leafing through it. There are hundreds of photos: me and my family in our hometown on the main avenue full of flowers, in a walk along the lake, on the beach, playing with Alex, then in a restaurant. The photos take on more color, when we moved to Italy. There are pictures of my wedding, the trips we had made with my mother: in Rimini, Como, Venice, and on the French Riviera.

I remain silent because I am moved to tears.

Diego is still standing by the door and is watching my reactions.

"But... how did you do this? Where did you get all these?"

"Don't you remember? You gave them to me long ago to turn them into digital photos. The others are from our camera."

I have never seen such a beautiful album, containing memories that can haunt you, giving you a rush of mixed emotions.

"Did you order it online?"

He nods his head.

"Thanks Diego. It is the best gift I have ever received."

I would have liked to add that I thought he was incapable of small gestures that fill your heart with joy, but words have lost their meaning.

Had he been like this even before but I hadn't noticed it? Or, having been forced to live like this, like inside a prison, made us closer?

I am still looking at the photos in the album. We were a really nice family. So much light in our smiles and so many dreams in our eyes!

In one photo there's me and Alex in bathing suits, thin, so alike, like twins. Our hands held a giant ball and we're laughing ... Other children would have quarreled because they had to share the few toys that existed at that time. But not the two of us...

Who could imagine that, in the years to come, we would become like strangers?

I leaf through the album again, but this time I'm distracted.

A thought keeps pestering me: Alex.

LOVE DECLARATION

I should call him, but I need to reflect first. I am quite certain that the messages from my mother and her desire to see us together have incited me.

I hesitate for an instant: do I call him from my mother's cell phone or from mine? Maybe he won't answer an unknown caller? Has he removed me from his contact list?

The cell phone rings and I wait. I have plenty of time, and I'm determined to hear his voice. Who knows how confused he will be when he will see mom's name on the screen.

"Hello."

"Hello Ale. It's me, Eva."

It was so long ago when I last uttered this name! This is how I called him when we were children: it was like a caress, an expression of unconditional love that bound us.

"Just as I thought."

"Did they inform you about mom?"

"Yes. These are terrible days to live. I would like to be there. When I left some time ago, I didn't know that I would never see her again."

Sobs choke his voice. I understand why Mom was so worried about him: he is so fragile!

"You couldn't have done anything even if you were here. Only when things will go back to normal will we be able to have the funeral."

He sighs. Then, his voice somewhat becomes lighter.

"Eva, I'm happy to talk to you. I have been waiting for this moment for years. Mom wanted the two of us ... "

"Yes I know. But I didn't call you only for mom, but also for myself. My life was missing an important piece: you."

"It is the same for me. Thank you. Someday we'll talk longer. Today I just want to tell you that ... I love you."

"I love you too."

The call ends, as if, after that statement, all other words spoken thereafter would be dull and meaningless.

FRIEND REQUEST

Every afternoon I listen nonstop to the press conference of the Civil Protection. It is already mid-April, and the number of dead people continues to soar: 602 people in the last twenty-four hours.

Diego stays close to me, trying to attract my attention with a thousand little things so as not to see me sad. He invites me to watch movies on the channels that transmit them all day, he talks to me about memories of the past, about his parents and we realize that we have a lot in common. We often talk of the journeys we have made, as if we want to travel far away, at least in our imagination, and have all the freedom in the world despite the current state of affairs.

We talk about the cruise that we were supposed to do in Spain, which has now been canceled. We dreamed of it for a long time. How excited I was when they sent us the booking details, accompanied by images of *MSC* ship. It was as big as a city, with all its comforts, with swimming pools, gyms, bars and restaurants. It would have been a beautiful and unforgettable experience. But now ... everything seems so distant.

If only all these were just a nightmare! The future is a question mark, the present is exhausting. I live with the memory of my mother and with the hope that, one day, we can bring her to her final resting place.

I no longer dream of traveling to exotic islands, but of an everyday life where I can enjoy the little things.

I continue reading painful stories of people whose hearts are not at peace due to the fact that they have not been able to be near to relatives during the days of their illness and in the last moments of their lives. Like me.

While I scroll through Facebook, a friend request attracts my attention. We have no mutual friends and his name doesn't mean anything to me. He has sent me a short message: *I would like to be one of your friends. We know each other, but you certainly don't remember me.*

I look at his profile, his gray hair, wrinkles on his face like deep furrows and accept his friend request. Without knowing that, from now on, my life will change.

WAITING FOR MY MOTHER

I started to write my thoughts on the computer, the impressions and the sufferings of the past months. When we open our heart to someone and share our concerns, we feel much better, but this does not happen with the one who has been with me for hours. In front of the white computer screen, I could empty my soul with all my sufferings yet it still remains passive and unfeeling.

I write and memories that I thought were forgotten and stored in a corner of my mind come rushing back and draw forth other memories.

Once, Alex and I were waiting for our mother. We were sitting on the school stairs; she had promised that she would come and get us. We knew how much she loved us and we were sure that she would appear at any moment, more beautiful than ever.

The school seemed deserted. My brother's restless gaze searched for her in the direction of the road and then he looked at me.

"Mom forgot about us," he whispered to me in a frightened voice.

I brought him close to me and hugged him. He wore a white shirt and blue shorts which made him look thinner. At dusk, our shadows spread over the ground and we shivered from the cold or maybe it was from the thought that mom wasn't coming to fetch us.

Suddenly, in the alley in front of us, a tall man appeared, his hair blowing in the wind. His shirt had printed squares all over it and he was wearing a pair of beige trousers. He came near us and only then did we recognize him: it was Dad.

None of us made the slightest move.

"Aren't you going back home?" he asked.

"We are waiting for mom."

The image of our mother bringing us home from school was so ingrained in our minds that other variations from this seem unthinkable. We were still looking in the direction where she would usually come from, in the hope that she would appear with her long hair and her beautiful smile.

She would be in a hurry to reach us immediately because of her love for us.

Dad, whom we hadn't seen for a long time, was stunned by our indifference to what he said. He didn't speak for an instant, then he found the solution: "Your mom sent me to get you. Children, look what I have brought for both of you!" He showed us two large boxes of candies and cookies. Only then did we jump to our feet and ran towards him. My father's resonant laughter filled the air.

I stop writing and go out onto the balcony. I sit on the bench and a light breeze envelops me, making me feel cold. The sun is setting, having a last look at this woman, no, at this little girl who is still waiting for her mother.

BEHIND THE SCHOOL GATE

A year had passed by after Dad left us and was no longer a part of our lives. That night, mom and I were resting on the double bed. Alex liked to sleep alone, to show us that he was not afraid of anything.

Mom kept telling me about dad's trip which this time was longer than usual, then she told me that it was already late and we had to sleep. It was like a beautiful tale to calm me down and make me fall asleep. But there was something that didn't convince me: in her eyes I could see a glimmer of tears, which she tried to hide at all cost.

At the moment when our conversation was about to end, I blurted out: "Mom, dad hasn't gone far away."

"What do you mean love, I don't understand."

Her voice trembled slightly.

"When I go out to the courtyard with my friends, I sometimes see him."

"Where?" she interrupted me, unable to mask her curiosity.

"Behind the school gate."

My mother paused, as if trying to figure out if what I had just said was a fact or a child's invention.

"Surely you must be imagining things. If your dad had a chance, he would have met you."

I wanted to add that I had seen him several times, but I didn't know if this fact would have made her happy or would have upset her. Then words ran out or we just needed to think in silence.

Months and years passed and I no longer expected to see my father. Gradually I got used to the absence and the emptiness that his abandonment had left in me. Mom always described him as a good parent. She told me that wherever he was, he was thinking of us, but surely he must have been in a difficult situation, from which he could not get out of. According to her, dad was happy with our accomplishments, like a spectator from afar, without becoming a central figure in our lives.

Like he was then, behind the school gate.

My mother was right. But I would only be convinced of this years later.

VICIOUS CYCLE

Alex and I now often communicate, but we still feel kind of shy with each other. We prefer to send each other text messages. Those years, in which we could not find a common ground, created a chasm between us. The approach will be slow, natural and perhaps we will be able to recreate that beautiful and innocent childhood memory.

One day I received an email from him: I read it in one breath. He is my brother, but in many ways he is still a stranger to me. I don't know his way of thinking, of reasoning, his feelings and emotions.

The lines he wrote to me confirmed some of my suspicions; on the other hand, they revealed to me a gentle and caring brother, as my mother frequently said.

Dear Eva, I apologize for the time I failed to understand you and your love. I don't know why I was so grumpy with you; at the beginning it was just the idea that when you find someone to love, you would distance yourself away from me and our relationship would not be the same as before. When I learned the identity of your boyfriend, I wanted to protect you at all cost from the dark and criminal world that he represented. I thought that if dad was part of our lives, such a thing would never have happened, so I tried to replace him. But nothing justifies my transformation into a brother-master, my severity and brutality. I turned into your worst opponent. Every time I accounted you for your actions, every time I tried to hide my fears behind arrogance, I knew that I was losing you little by little.

We had been so close before! We had guessed every doubt, every insecurity that one or the other felt without needing to speak but, suddenly, we were living a reality full of conflicts and we got lost in its vortex.

Something was wrong with my behavior, so I tried to fight that other person: I drank alcohol to forget. Things got worse: I raised my voice against you or against mom, entering a vicious circle from which it was impossible to get out. Mom always forgave me, while you didn't: you got angry, you went away and the distance between us became insurmountable.

I feel pain because our mother has not been able to live to this day, but I am convinced that in her most beautiful dreams she has seen us thousands of times chatting calmly, trying to build a new brother-sister relationship, in whose veins flows the same blood.

FORGIVING

Dear Ale! Many years ago, when I discovered the true nature of my love, I wanted to cry and scream. Until then I had lived with the disappointment of our father's absence, who although was not present every day, was my joy and my safety. Then, the disappointment doubled. Mom was always close to me, but she also had to calm down the waves of your anger.

We were a family of four who eventually drifted away from each other. Up to a certain point I justified your actions, because I too felt that rancor and hatred towards the person who had filled me with the promise of eternal love and perpetual happiness. I had lived with my eyes closed and, once they were open, the world was no longer the same.

I was too focused on my pain, on my desperation to understand you even a little bit. However, aggression and arrogance are unacceptable even when they come from someone who is part of the family. Today I am able to recognize your drama and above all ... to forgive you.

We had to lose the dearest person, our mother, to reconnect again. With her death, she gave us the most powerful lesson she could give us.

I don't want to dwell on the past. For weeks we have been locked up at home and I realize how fragile life is, how adorable are the everyday things that we can't do now: a walk in the park, by the sea, sipping a cup of coffee while contemplating the fiery sunset, a carefree conversation with strangers….

When we were in Albania we knew how to give weight and meaning to these 'trifles', probably because we couldn't afford the big things. We were satisfied with less. At that time the fridge was not full, nor were the shelves, but we had affection and thousands of memories that filled our hearts.

Here, everything seems possible: luxury, abundance, wealth, a life without limits and our existence has been transformed into a crazy rush towards money, the material aspect. We live together under the same roof but it is each for himself, because the self is more important; our separate lives divide us and transform us into strangers.

NOSTALGIA

Today is Easter. Diego starts the day by cooking. He prepares fruit salad (I don't know what it has to do with the feast), then the lamb with potatoes: he pours some oil and wine, then he fills it with spices, another of his passions. I peel the potatoes, and I take care of the programming of the oven. In a nutshell, I'm basically not doing anything.

Memories continue to haunt me. Wherever I turn my head I see them, touch them and talk to them.

A year ago, Mom was with us. I remember that she was telling us fragments of my childhood when, as soon as she mentioned dad's name, her voice broke with emotion. She immediately changed subject, starting to describe a small incident that had happened to her a few days earlier. She had taken the wrong bus to come home and had gone to the outskirts of the city. She had asked the driver for information, but she could not understand his explanations. She wasn't sad about it; in fact, she was happily contemplating that part of the city that she had never visited, thus satisfying her curiosity. The two of us laughed, but my thoughts were somewhere. I wondered if the tears in her eyes were for Dad. Had she loved him so much? Even if he had left her for another woman?

How much strength and love does it take not to blame a man who has turned his back on you? Surely, she still loved him. Not only that, but deep within herself, where everyone guards their most intimate feelings, she was still waiting for some news, some sign from him. Though she had aged and her passions had faded, she still waited for him. It means that ... we never stop loving.

I would like to have a love like that too. Mom never revealed that part of her soul submerged in the shadows because she only wanted to project hope and positivity to us. Or perhaps that part of her didn't exist?

A wonderful aroma fills the air. Diego asks me if I want to drink wine, but I shake my head to say *no*. He seems to understand my feelings.

"Eva, don't feel too guilty. Drink only a little bit of wine. Your mother has always dreamed of your happiness."

I hand him the glass and try to free myself from the sorrow that has engulfed me.

This room today is full of images and memories of mom.

Diego lightly caresses my face: "The persons we love who are no longer among us always remain in our hearts."

I would like to say a tender word to him, but I can't. I hold back the tears. My sadness slowly fades away, replaced by nostalgia.

EFINITIONS

Diego and I have never said 'I love you' to each other. It was he who made me change my opinion on the citizens of this beautiful country, the Italians, whom I imagined all as passionate, who filled you with nice words and compliments.

We had been engaged for a few months when I had to travel to Albania. I arrived in Bari and had just boarded the *NGV* ferry when he called me. Surprisingly, we talked longer than the other times, about a quarter of an hour, and when I was about to say goodbye, he said *I miss you*. This word was so unusual in our vocabulary that I doubted I heard it well, perhaps due to the strong wind or the sound of the sea waves, so I asked him to repeat it. In fact, I did right, because years had to pass before I could hear it again.

Love for me was passion, that strong impulse to want to know the other beyond all limits; and when the fire goes out, at least the embers still remain.

One day I asked Diego what definition he gave to this sentiment. Though he considers himself a pragmatist, he doesn't like philosophical discussions at all. He didn't answer right away and looked away at a distant point. Maybe I should have asked him this question the day before to get the answer just in those moment.

While I was waiting, I thought that love, obviously, was not the lack of beautiful words or declarations of love as is the case with the two of us.

Finally, Diego spoke and it took me some time to decipher his interpretation.

"Love is not words, gestures and compliments, but a journey for two towards the same destination."

I wanted to object, but I am convinced that in this world there is also room for my husband's judgments, especially when they are so rare.

Years have passed since then.

If someone now asks me what *love* is, I would not answer *passion, that strong impulse to want to know the other beyond all limits,* but simply *the presence of someone who warms your soul and heart more than a hug; it is the division of a tear in two.*

CHILD, FOR AN INSTANT

I go out to buy some bread. Diego tells me I need some fresh air, so this time I'm going. My legs hurt and I can hardly walk.

There are several shops in the main square of the area where we live, but they are closed. Only one of them is open.

I am surprised that there are so many people waiting outside in line that the queue reached up to a small garden. I was standing near a tree.

When I went to work or downtown, I met an elderly lady at the bus stop who immediately started a conversation with me. She told me about her children, her grandchildren and, above all, about the buses that were so unreliable. Five minutes later I had already forgotten her life story. Now we meet again: it seems like years have passed since the last time I saw her.

We greet each other with our eyes, but she has not forgotten her old habits. She approaches me and starts talking about the virus and the many victims in the city. I don't understand her well because of her mask, but I try to guess. What else can we talk about in these crazy times?

I agree with her about everything; I want to say my opinion but then all I do is utter sounds that cannot be interpreted and just resemble animal grunts. She keeps talking and has no intention of stopping. I find a moment in which she is looking away and inadvertently avoid her. When she realizes that I am no longer there to listen to her, she, without getting discouraged, approaches someone else.

I have forgotten how to communicate. Fear and desperation have overwhelmed me and being close to someone makes me apprehensive. Does it happen to other people too?

According to statistics, the number of victims has decreased: it has gone down to 282. But behind this figure, there are hundreds of families who have lost their loved ones.

Tomorrow is May 1st. The sky is dark and there is fog; the rain starts and stops as if someone up there is giving orders to it. I recall the first of Mays of my childhood, the new clothes that my mother kept folded in the drawer, the light plastic sandals and the walks on the boulevard, where the bright colors of the perfumed flowers seemed to mock the paper flowers I held in my hands.

I would like to transform myself into a child for a moment: be surrounded by my parents' love, protected from the cruelties of the world, to see all the colors of the universe which, at this very moment, I cannot distinguish one from the other.

TEMPORARY PEACE

It was difficult to determine what I felt exactly after the abortion. On one hand, I was casual and carefree because the bond with Fabio was forever broken. I thought that the future was mine, that I could make all my dreams come true and that surely, somewhere, in a corner of the world, someone who would love me with all his soul, was waiting for me. I had rejected that child, consciously knowing that he would grow up without a father and with a problematic parent. This would have meant giving him a difficult childhood which I have experienced, or much worse than that.

But my peace was only temporary. Whenever I saw a child taking his first steps on the street, running, laughing or playing ball in the park, they seemed to me beautiful images like those found in postcards and my heart ached at such a sight.

Perhaps my baby would also be that age. I found myself counting with my fingers the months, the years and in front of my eyes I saw a blond girl with blue eyes, with a beautiful smile like the rainbow, while I prepared her for school. I combed her hair, I made her wear a pleated skirt and a white shirt. It wasn't long before it dawned on me that these episodes belonged to another mother, to another life. Then sadness became a part of me and the idea of having saved that being from a bad fate did not reassure me at all. I felt bad; guilt and remorse poisoned my day.

When I knew Diego, we dedicated ourselves to getting to know each other and to cultivate our passions. We also never seriously talked about having a baby because I didn't feel any maternal instinct or because leafing through that chapter of my life caused me pain. Had the abortion killed that desire in me? Or did I feel that way because I had deprived a creature of the right to live, and I thought that I could never be a devoted mother?

I hoped to be free from the tormenting thoughts, but they came back as powerful as a hurricane every time I didn't expect them, destroying my peace and carrying it away.

THE GIFTS

The stranger by the name of Andy, whose friendship I accepted a few days ago, sent me a message. Its lines seemed to me like rays of light that penetrate the fog and illuminate the surroundings.

Hello Eva, thanks for your friendship! I wish I had your phone number to be able to talk longer, but if you don't trust me or don't feel comfortable, I understand you.

I want to tell you a few things that I hope will convince you that I am a close friend of your family and not just someone who wants to spend time browsing the internet.

I know you since you were a little girl. Your mother said that you were a quiet child: you respected the hours of eating and sleeping and she loved you from the very moment she held you in her arms.

The older you grew, the more you looked like her: with long straight hair, black and dreamy eyes. You were sweet and obedient. When your dad told you fragments of his travels, you didn't ask questions. You stared into space, imagining those straight or winding roads that led to a world that you could only visit by imagination.

When your brother was born, you didn't feel any jealousy, as it usually happens with other children. He was for you a toy, a form of amusement, and afterwards, a friend. You grew up together and every time he played a prank, you didn't tell it to your parents, but instead, tried to hide it.

When your father returned from his travels after a long time, you did not run towards him, but you waited for him to come to you and hug you. You did not show your feelings, you were shy and withdrawn, while your brother had no difficulty in showing them.

One evening, when your father came home and the first thing he did was to pull out the gifts, all of a sudden, you said to him: "I don't want gifts!"

He was left speechless. He had never seen you angry. "I just want you to stay here, with us," you added.

You turned your back on him, and your parents, after a moment of embarrassment, burst out laughing.

One day, your father realized you were right. Gifts - toys, clothes or perfumes - had no value at all, while the presence of someone and the affection in the family enhanced your life.

Before continuing, I wanted to ask you if these episodes remind you of anything.

FRAGILE BALANCE

Those lines brought back forgotten feelings: emotion, nostalgia, anxiety. I see myself playing with Alex or waiting for a hug from dad. I remember the gifts, his laughter that filled the house with joy as soon as he crossed the threshold. In fact, my mother told me that I never woke up at night and that I hadn't caused her any worries during my childhood. She didn't tell me this to point out that that happened when I grew up. It was me who often asked her about the past, about those fragments that had not been able to occupy a space in my memory.

It is possible that Andy is a friend of my family, but I don't want to have a conversation with him, or tell him if I remember those events or not, if they move me or make me nostalgic. If I have been a reserved child, now, without a doubt, I remain a woman who does not like to open up to strangers or express her deepest feelings.

I have experienced the same reservation with Diego and this may have been the cause of some misunderstandings. I did not tell him about my fears and the insecurities that came from a distant past, because it seemed to portray me as someone fragile and this would not have helped the relationship. I was afraid that he would judge me and would not continue the acquaintance with me.

Lately, I have talked with him like never before about the difficult relationship with my ex-boyfriend and the abortion. I felt liberated, reborn.

One day, he said to me: "Eva, it seems to me I know you today".

The two of us have stopped the frenzied rush of everyday life, even if compelled by greater forces, and we have reflected on our relationship, as we have not done for a long time.

I'm trying to find a balance with Diego, with my brother but, above all, with myself so as not to let the pain overwhelm me and hold my life hostage. I don't want this fragile balance to be ruined by a stranger's messages.

UNFULFILLED PROMISE

Your father told me that you had a doll with straight black hair. You wanted to make the hair grow and make it the same as yours. With the passage of time you got nervous: "How come the hair isn't getting long?" You sat on the sofa and talked with it constantly.

Your father couldn't figure out the fact that you talked more to the doll than to him. He was saddened by the distance that had been created between you. He felt guilty for not being an exemplary father, even though it was work that forced him to stay away from you. Every time he came home, the toys scattered here and there - the dolls, the cars, the stuffed animals - reminded him of his absences in the family, and seemed to blame him. He bought them to apologize for not being present in your daily life, but also to gain your attention and affection.

One day, Alex had begged him not to go on a long journey but to accompany him to school; he replied that he couldn't. Your brother had gone into a corner of the living room, covered his face with his palms, and started to cry.

It seemed that the teacher had punished him for some trouble in the classroom.

Your father laughed about it but Elena took him aside and explained everything to him. Alex was bullied by his classmates, they told him that he didn't have a father, otherwise they would have seen him somewhere: at school, on the street, at the bar. Whenever your brother opened his mouth to say something, they made fun of him. Your father's heart was broken.

Then he went to Alex, put a hand on his shoulder and, turning Alex towards him, said: "Son, I promise you I'll take you to school next time!"

He wanted to add that, in this way, his friends would be convinced that he really existed, but he did not say anything more. He took him in his arms and hugged him, feeling all the weight of guilt on his chest.

Your father never managed to fulfill that promise....

THE IDEA OF FREEDOM

I don't want to bore you with detailed descriptions, but maybe you would like to read them.

I learned from a post of yours that your mother has passed away. I am so sorry, I knew her well. That beautiful, noble, exemplary, generous woman ... I see her image in front of me.

I had a long conversation with your father one day. We were sitting in the usual bar facing the lake; the wind was blowing and the water was rough and full of waves. The sky had turned gray, announcing the coming of the storm, and pigeons flew in the air, frightened.

We were having beer together. Your father looked worried. He was more silent than usual, he couldn't find the right words. He stared at the glass of beer and moved it nervously on the table, distracted. I didn't understand what preoccupied him. Finally, he opened up to me.

He had known another woman: smiling, lively, casual, without prejudice. He liked her because she was as free as the air, without children, without a family. When they were together, he did not condemn himself, he had no sense of guilt, and he was serene and happy. Together, they could plan all the trips they wanted, there were no children to think of, no tears, no sleepless nights, no responsibilities.

This woman represented his idea of being free, out of the family prison. She invited him, seduced him to tread other roads and say "no" to a life full of sacrifices he had led up to that moment. He had experienced new sensations, which made him look at the world with optimism. Despite being forty-three, this seemed to him like a new beginning, full of curiosity and surprises. But he was torn between two passions, and, obviously, he couldn't go on like this.

That love story coincided with the collapse of the political system in the country, with the beginning of an era that gave you complete freedom to escape from the old clichés and embrace the new. That's how he understood things.

At that moment when everyone was trying to leave the country, he abandoned his family. It seemed like an easy solution, but the difficulties would arise later.

He stayed in the city for a while. He went to your school several times, watching you both from afar. Once he told me that you saw him for a few seconds, and then you joined your friends. He didn't have the courage to call you. What could he have said to an innocent child, what explanations could he give her when he himself did not know exactly what he would do and what awaited him in the future?

People accused him, glared at him, until one night they both crossed the border to go to the neighboring country, Greece. There was no day in which he did not think of you, that he did not dream of returning only to meet you, but the everyday life was ruthless and suffocated his dreams.

He was an illegal alien, did not have a residence permit and could not travel. He was struggling to survive, and the hope that one day he would return was sometimes strong and sometimes fragile.

He had imagined a worry-free, calm, happy life, but he hadn't calculated how much he would miss you.

He followed you from afar. He knew very well that you could not afford to continue your studies. He decided to save money and help you but ... a sudden event would have overturned his plans.

IN THIS CHAOS

I can't control the flow of my thoughts and emotions. This stranger's bond with my family has been truly special.

I remember well that black-haired doll, one of the most beautiful relics of my childhood, which has withstood the test of time. It was a gift from dad and represents that short and tender moment that will never come back.

When I saw my father behind the school gate I was shocked. I didn't expect him there, but on the threshold of our home. In those moments, I preferred to continue the game I played with my friends and not face him. I knew that he had gone out from my mother's life, from ours and something had changed forever. My mother's melancholic eyes, that emptiness that my father's departure had left in my soul and that surely would never be filled, followed me everywhere. It was the empty chair at the table, the walks that we could no longer take together, his absent embrace, the incomplete image of the family, but above all, the radical change in my brother's character.

How is it possible that I don't remember this person, even though he was close to my family? Was I too young then or perhaps he didn't often come to our house? He appeared at this very moment, in this chaos, just when I'm in a constant duel with pain, telling me truths about our lives that no one else knows and that are the greatest comfort to me. They bring my mother's memory closer to me and I'm glad that another person found her unique, not just me.

About dad, um ... I don't know what to say. Over the years I never wished him to be happy with that other woman. I couldn't bear thinking about my mother's life, full of sacrifices and the suffering that Alex and I experienced.

I answer Andy laconically.

Hi, thanks for the messages. They remind me of fragments of my past. It's strange, but I don't remember you. I don't know exactly what place you occupy in my parents' life. I just want to tell you that, in these moments, your messages seem like a gentle breeze that calm my soul. The only thing left from my parents are the memories and I will keep them inside of me in my every step.

Diego does not take this correspondence seriously. While I constantly analyze and think about every detail, my husband only sees it as a good way to take care of something and not despair.

Alex tells me that the situation in Spain is normalizing.

"Please, when they'll let you know about mom ... I definitely want to be there to give her the last farewell."

"Surely," I stammer and her absence becomes stronger and more real.

Life will find its rhythm but mom will no longer be here. Soon the bars and restaurants will open, but we won't meet to talk for hours over a cup of coffee. What I would give to have her near!

The days are getting longer and warmer, the colors brighter and the sky bluer, but I don't know if the sun will be able to dry the tears of my city.

LABYRINTHS

Your father's only dream was to obtain a residence permit. After a few months he had an appointment at the police station. If all went well, he would make the trip to his hometown. Years had passed and you were no longer children. He would have liked to talk to you and your mother Elena, to apologize for his sudden departure, for the many problems and troubles she had faced alone. He wasn't sure you would forgive him, you had every reason not to, but he hoped for your understanding and empathy.

In a bedroom drawer he saved money each month and put it in an envelope. He often counted it and felt satisfied: that sum brought him closer to the goal he had set. He wanted to give you a gift, help you get on with school or satisfy any wish. He imagined that beautiful, exciting journey, like when he came home from work, when he showed up on the doorstep, when he hugged you and your happiness touched the sky. He could not know that that evening would completely change the course of events.

The bus that was taking him from Omonia square in the suburb of Athens, where he lived in a small rented apartment with Bianca, his love, was almost empty. From time to time you could see a few passengers with grim faces like him, wearing old, wrinkled clothes, with lowered eyelids and with their bodies swaying here and there with every movement of the vehicle.

The city slept while the shop lights that went on and off tried to disprove this fact. In a normal, everyday life, in which the long hours of construction work exhausted him, wherein a part of his soul was missing, he rejoiced at the idea that he would soon lie down and fall asleep, only to wake up again the next day at four o'clock in the morning.

When he entered his apartment, Bianca talked incessantly; it seemed that something was hidden behind that stream of words. But he was too tired even to greet her.

He sat down at the table and began to eat in silence, without looking into her eyes, without following her monologue; he murmured "hmm" to give her the impression that he was listening.

After some minutes he could not utter a single syllable, a sound, as if he were in front of an abstract, intricate frame, with labyrinths that lead you nowhere nor to any path you want to take.

IN THE TRAP

"I want to tell you something," Bianca said to your father with an unusual glint in her eyes.

"It would be better for us to talk tomorrow, I just want to sleep now."

But her wife shook her head in denial.

"Tomorrow you will be just as tired and reluctant to listen to me."

Um, in the end she was right. What distinguished one day from another? Maybe the news that came from Albania or what they heard from that foreign country.

He stared at her. Bianca put a hand on her abdomen and began to caress it with slow and rhythmic movements. This gesture was not alien to him. He understood everything, words were superfluous. He felt the need to take a deep breath. He needed to go out again, wander the deserted streets of the Greek capital, collect his thoughts, or rather, himself.

"Anton, the two of us are expecting a baby!"

He could not smile or become part of her joy.

"You had told me you didn't want children." And the echo of his voice made him realize that there were no notes of sweetness there. On the contrary, he was rude, angry, accusing.

"I thought so, but now it's different. I can say with full conviction that I want this creature with all my soul."

She was waiting for him to tell her that it was the same for him too, that he was happy that now they would be a real family, but the only sentence he had uttered was: "I have two other children."

"Oh, they're already adults and don't need you anymore."

He wanted to oppose her, tell her that children always need their parents, that he had obligations towards them, that because of his fault they had lived a troubled childhood, but he remained silent.

He had not yet turned fifty but he felt old, too old to have a child and in a trap. He had loved that woman for her character, for her passion, for the way she held herself, dressed, combed her hair, but more for the fact that she had admitted to him that she did not want children and that they would be free to live, to have fun, to travel, that is, to do the things that he had not been able to with his family.

He naively hoped that she would change her mind, that this mistake would be corrected and that they would be as happy as before.

"We will have a lot of expenses and I don't know if we will be able to afford them."

She looked at him slyly. "You have been careful and in all these years you have managed to save. Don't forget the envelope in the drawer."

Anton would have liked to scream, vent the anger that those words provoked in him, and say to her: "Oh, no, you won't touch that envelope, it's not for you," but he couldn't. He shook his head helplessly, as if what he was experiencing was a frightening dream, a nightmare that kept him from opening his mouth and uttering a single syllable.

He got up, shuffling on his feet, and went to the bathroom. He took off his clothes one by one, tossed them on the cold floor and started showering. Dozens of streams of water wet his face and there he cried like a child for all the dreams that were dissolving in front of his eyes, without mercy.

OUR ANNIVERSARY

Diego reminds me that today is the anniversary of our wedding. He has become more attentive and it seems to me that I'm getting to know him more and more. I continue to feel lost from the death of mom and of various events that have been happening lately. I'm looking for answers that no one can give me.

Diego goes out to buy fresh bread and I close the door behind him. Suddenly the phone rings. It's Alex and he sounds excited. He tells me that he remembers this date from many years ago, when I wore the white dress. "Congratulations and be happy, *sister*."

I get emotional. I have forgotten how sweet this word was.

The sun shines through the raised shutters and light fills the house. Under the strong rays of the sun, the wooden bench on the balcony seems to be dressed in gold. It is the place where I used to sit with mom. God knows how much I miss her!

Diego comes back and his hands are loaded with things. In one, he holds something with extreme caution, fearing it might fall.

"It's our anniversary cake," he says with a laugh.

Slowly, I open the container. The cake is so beautiful that I almost regret having to eat it: with white cream, strawberries and the number ten in the center. Amazing how the years go by!

It would be nice if we have mom with us.

I try to chase this thought away, because I don't want to fill our anniversary with tears.

Diego takes the lasagna out of the oven, and hot steam covers him. He pours wine into my glass and its drops splash on my face. We make a toast.

"Gëzuar," he says me in my language.

I don't have time to congratulate him on the dish he has cooked, because he has already eaten it all and is now standing up. He is a speed champion.

We have spent sunny and foggy days in this city, we've shared our thoughts, passions and problems. Diego, although he gives you the impression of being a difficult and impetuous person, always advises me to be calm, to take people for who they are, without trying to change them and without expecting anything in return.

He sits down and waits for me to finish the food.

"Eva, I want to tell you something."

"Me too, but you start."

I notice his smile, which has conquered me from the very first moment of our acquaintance. This time he looks at me and not at the four walls of the apartment. I'm impatient, waiting for him to say the first word.

FOR MANY MORE YEARS (DIEGO)

A few days before the lockdown, I asked you for a break because I needed to reflect. Our relationship had become cold and formal and we hardly exchanged a few words. In the evening, the only time we could meet each other, we were both tense and tired, but not of arguing. The house was not a safe haven, but a place that couldn't give me peace and tranquility.

Isolation, being close for a long time, as we would never have been in normal conditions, helped us to be more attuned to each other, without the usual rush, without the anxieties of everyday life.

I leafed through the memories, the trips we made around the world and I remembered what we used to be, the genuine feelings and infinite joy, that desire to have adventures and to laugh. I had to start right there to get to know you and understand you better.

Never like before have I understood your story, the sad moments you had with your family, the tears you shed.

I didn't know what it meant to leave your country and move to another, where you don't know anyone, not even the language. I didn't know what it meant to leave behind a part of your soul, of your life, to try to establish roots in another land and how much courage and persistence it took for this.

I have not been able to read the frequent changes in your mood, your insistence on pursuing happiness even in a foreign land. I have not even been able to notice your tendency to write, the desire to throw into the computer that baggage of feelings, worries and sufferings that, for various reasons, you could not share with me. I was unable to decipher those episodes of the past that I called *strange*, without being able to find a name for them: when you were moved every time we walked on Lake of Garda and stared at the flight of the seagulls, when you sat on the shore and collected shells, your dreams, uttering words in your mother tongue.

I got to know you better through the pain, the tears, and your silence, the inclination to forgive the mistakes of your family members and live in harmony. Tears will help you see the future clearly. I promise you that I will be by your side for many more years, God willing.

"I love you!"

"Me too," I whisper.

The anxieties and worries vanish somewhere far away.

ON THE THRESHOLD OF A HOUSE

Your father led a life that left him with enough room to think only about the present. His days now were filled with the baby's cries, with his first steps, with those joys and emotions, but also stress and worries that he had once felt and that he never imagined would be repeated.

The images of the past no longer tormented him.

The memory of you existed, but it was placed in a corner of his heart. He focused on the life of his child, whom he began to love little by little, day after day, enjoying with him all the moments that he had not been able to enjoy with his other children.

He came home every evening, he could caress him and play with him whenever he wanted, he could say 'goodnight' and whisper to him tender words of love.

He was asking acquaintances and friends about you, but it was not easy to know some things. The city was deserted, thousands had emigrated and others dreamed of fleeing. After much effort, someone gave him the cellular number of your mother, Elena. He kept that piece of paper in his pocket for a long time, without daring to make a call. He was afraid to hear her voice, he knew that a 'forgive me' would be insufficient to restore her lost peace, to make him look like an exemplary husband and father, whom the waves of life had sent far away. One day, when he dared to call, the number became non-existent.

Over time, communicating with his family was no longer a priority. He just needed to know that his children had grown up and things were going well. Or that was what he wanted to believe.

He finally did that long desired journey and decided to knock on his old house. His heart was beating fast, like that of a teenager in the presence of his first love.

He walked nostalgically through the streets, along the coast of the lake, and collected memories, composed of games, hugs, attempts to teach you how to swim and other things that he could not recall because they were too unimportant and the wind had taken them away.

When he found himself in front of the house, he stopped for a few moments to regain the strength he needed to knock on that door, on that threshold that he hadn't crossed in what seemed like a lifetime.

THE CHAINS OF MARRIAGE

Life had tried to deprive him of this moment, giving him so many problems and difficulties, but he had faced them all. He felt like he was an unwanted guest and he hoped it wasn't too late.

The flowers were beautiful, as they were then. Careful hands had watered them and planted more. A wonderful scent filled the air. While he waited, deep in thought, he looked at the small windows (like a doll's house) - the white curtains, embroidered on the sides - and he lived with the illusion that nothing had changed, that time had stood still and that his children would appear, noisy and joyful before him. He saw Elena with her arms across her chest, her hair caressed by the wind, while she scolded them with a smile: "Slowly, because dad is tired!"

Suddenly, someone he had never seen before, a man of about sixty years old, appeared. What was this man doing in his house?

"Whom are you looking for?" the stranger asked.

"Elena," he replied, and for a moment he thought that this man had probably taken his place.

A silent rage hit his chest. He glared at him, but it didn't last long. What right did he have to appear after many years and control the lives of the people he himself had abandoned?

"There is no Elena living here."

"It is not possible. She is a woman with two small children, excuse me, two adults. The daughter must be..."

He tried to calculate the years, but he couldn't and he stood there as if lost.

"We bought this house some time ago."

"Oh," was all he could say. The stranger's words had the strength of a slap.

"Surely it will have been a good opportunity."

The stranger did not speak. He did not understand what this eccentric guest, who still stood there, looking helpless, meant. After a pause he added: "Yes, the landlady was in a hurry, she was going to Italy with her children. They had no money and wanted to sell it as soon as possible."

He swallowed and felt a stab in the heart. The house, full of memories, joy and pain, where the children had taken their first steps, where they had cried and rejoiced, had been sold for a small sum of money.

The stranger on the other side of the door, where he once stayed, spoke again: "They say that the owner of the house abandoned the family because he found another woman. He didn't even want to know about his children anymore. Do you understand how superficial we men are at times?"

Your father nodded. He knew very well the man who had left his family to free himself from the chains of marriage and try to be happy. But if someone had asked him what color happiness was, he could not have described it.

He said goodbye, muttering something between his teeth, and, with wobbly legs, he took a path that he did not know where it would lead him. His shoulders were hunched, the weight of guilt weighed heavily upon them.

NO ONE ABANDONS HIS LAND (EVA)

I have before my eyes our house, the small garden where I played with my brother, the window, behind which I looked the storms. Sometimes I would stick my face so hard on the smooth surface of glass that my mother told me to be careful not to stain it. On the mist that I formed with my breath, I wrote the initials of our names.

I feel the pain my mother felt when she had to sell it, because together with Alex they were going to travel to Italy. Um, they didn't have enough money even for the travel. She told me that she often dreamed of that building, heard our light footsteps on the floor, imagined our father leafing noisily through the newspaper and the door that was always open for the people.

On one of our trips from Italy to our city, my mom asked me to pass through the alleyway of our home that now was no longer ours.

"Mom, but what's the point?"

"When it comes to nostalgia, it all makes sense, my daughter."

She stopped in front of the gate: she looked wistfully at every flower and every blade of grass. I wanted to look into her eyes, read her feelings, but she wore her sunglasses, so it wasn't easy for me.

We stayed there, for who knows how long. I patted her on the back, as if I wanted to cheer her up: "Mom, come on! Let's go now."

But she was still inside those walls, in that life that had once given her happiness and pain and where, surely if she could, she would go back to live again.

I pulled her lightly by the arm and with a low voice, without any notes of enthusiasm, she said: "No one abandons his land, my daughter. In Italy, we live better than here, but there we remain anonymous. I would have preferred to eat less and stay here, at my home." Then, as if remembering that melancholy and sadness did not fit her, she added: "The important thing is that I am close to you. I would have followed you even to the most remote place in the world."

The ringing of the phone interrupts my memories. The voice seems to be recorded and it takes me some time to realize that it's not. I'm informed that on the 2nd of June we will be able to hold my mother's funeral ceremony at the Bergamo cemetery. She explains to me that the number of accompanying persons must be limited. When she is ready to hang up, I tell her: "Sorry, but there is a problem. My mother's last wish was to be buried in her hometown in Albania."

THE MAGIC IS ELSEWHERE

Diego starts working tomorrow. A good part of the businesses and establishments will open. It is the dawn after the devastating hurricane season.

This beginning excites me. I was so close to my husband during this period that I feel like we've always been like that. For an instant I am afraid that the daily routine will again take him away from me or that it will snatch the most beautiful part of him that I have recently discovered: the calm and the desire to talk.

But then I don't think about it anymore.

After dinner we stay on the balcony. Diego holds a bottle of Peroni beer in his hand while I have a glass of water with a thin slice of lemon. The sky displays an infinite number of colors: gray, orange and red. The clouds try to cover the sun, but it just seems to float between them.

This twilight hides many mysteries. Our bodies close to each other, the touch of our hands, the silent voices that hang deep in the air and the nostalgia for those who are no longer among us.

But there is also something else that Diego doesn't know.

"I told you about the person I often communicate with, the friend of my family."

"Yes, I remember that."

"You won't believe it."

"What happened?"

"He expressed the desire to be present during my mother's funeral. I didn't answer him. This request seems strange to me. What do you think?"

Diego looks at me and then casts his gaze towards the horizon, as if this would help him give the correct answer.

"I'm convinced, like you, that he knew your parents well. Hmm. What can I tell you? Let him come."

"Ah, I forgot. He told me that he will bring me something important that belonged to both of them."

"What could it be?"

"If you only knew how curious I am. But I have my doubts regarding all this. What he writes to me is true, at least the episodes I remember. But ... if he knew my dad so well, if he was by his side in the most difficult moments - as he tells me - how is it possible that now he doesn't know where he is and has lost contact with him?"

The sound of an incoming message distracts me and I quickly pick up the phone. Alex has written to me: *Finally! I'll be back in a week. I am satisfied and excited, as if I were stepping on that soil for the first time.*

I too write him a few words: *We are waiting for you.*

I get up, leave my cell phone in the kitchen and sit next to Diego.

"I want to tell you something. In fact, I tried to tell you a few days ago, but now I'm completely convinced ... I'm pregnant."

Diego whirls around. Twilight has lost its colors, its beauty. The magic is now elsewhere. He looks at me as if he's waiting for me to tell him I'm kidding, that you can't get pregnant at my age, but I'm silent.

"And ... what have you decided?"

His voice breaks, a tear lurking behind his eyes.

"I'll keep it. For me, for both of us, for mom."

"This is the best news you have given me in all these years."

He throws his arms around my neck and in his big warm embrace there is also room for a child.

T THE AIRPORT

When the plane arrives at the airport of Milano Malpensa, Diego and I are in the waiting room. The few people walking around wear masks on their faces and now this seems quite normal, as if we have been wearing them all our lives. I have imagined today's meeting hundreds of times and I feel sad at the thought that mother is not here and will never be with us again.

I recognize Alex, taller than the others: he has lost weight, his hair is becoming thinner or he has cut it short. He drags the suitcase and doesn't take his eyes off it and then he looks up. Our glances meet and he forgets the luggage, letting it crash to the ground noisily. Our laughter dissolves the tension that is palpable. Diego greets him and, without a word, lifts the suitcase, going towards the car.

We hug and burst into tears. In those tears there is the pain for the loss of mom, there are the years of distance, in which we hated each other; in those tears is our story: two unfortunate children abandoned by their father on an ordinary day, who had to live only with the memory of him.

We are still like this when Diego comes back and invites us for a drink. We order coffee, while Alex orders sandwich and Coke.

"I was very excited, I didn't put anything in my mouth." He is silent for a few seconds and then he asks me: "How did it happen?"

"So fast that I can't believe she's gone."

"I thought that if I were here, she wouldn't get sick. But none of these assumptions matter right now. Time does not go back. If this were possible, I too would have changed many things in my life."

"It's never too late."

"For mom, it is."

"Ale, I want you to meet a person. He appeared in the most difficult moments of my life, that is, immediately after the death of mom. I only know him from his photo."

"I don't understand. Is he here?"

"No, he'll be at the cemetery before we take our mother's coffin to Albania. But read these, these are his messages, I printed them. They will remind you of many family memories."

"Thank you. I really need to dive into the past and meet Mom there."

We sip our coffee and Alex apologizes to Diego for having talked to me for so long, keeping him on the sideline.

I get up to pay, look back and see how the two of them chat and smile. My husband pats him on the back and they look like two friends who have reunited after a long time. The ice has finally melted.

THE STRANGER

A tall, handsome man gets out of the taxi. He wears an elegant black suit and a white shirt; a boy of about twenty accompanies him. The wind plays with his gray hair and the wrinkles on his face indicate a life that has gone through ups and downs.

I know him immediately. I greet him and he comes to our direction. Alex and I are sitting in one of the bars on the road that leads to the cemetery.

There is something familiar about his face, in the attentive gaze that tries to fathom what the other thinks. I have seen him somewhere or I have this idea simply from his photo on the social network. I thank him for coming, but he is the one who thanks us for giving him the opportunity to be here today.

"This is my brother Alex."

He nods his head, as if to say 'I know'.

He looks excited, almost shocked. He takes off his jacket and nervously moves his hands, which are crisscrossed by large veins. He orders coffee and a bottle of water.

"I didn't think I'd arrive so late," he says in a shaking voice.

I try to tell him that it's not late, that we were supposed to be here at ten, but he touches my arm lightly as if to tell me to let him go on.

"Late because Elena is no longer among us. She was a unique woman, but she didn't find the man she deserved. I ... I realized that after I walked away. Her silence and her dignity amazed me. She never raised her voice to ask me for help on your behalf. She never cursed the day she met me, she never defiled our love. I learned - from the others - that she spoke as if one day I would come back, even though inside herself she was convinced of the opposite."

Tears relentlessly stream down my cheeks. In a faint voice I ask him: "So you're not a friend of the family, but ... dad?"

He confirms without looking us in the eye.

I want to tell him that I thought he was, that I suspected, or wanted to suspect.

"With the help of my son, I was able to register on the social network and I did so in the hope of finding you. Andy Alevan. The surname is the union of: Ale and Eva. Not a day has gone by without me thinking about you. Maybe you will accept me in your life, maybe you will close the door on me. If it's the latter, I will understand; I would have done the same with a father who abandoned me and ruined the best years of my childhood. But today I needed to come. First, for Elena, to ask her to 'forgive me' and say goodbye', but also to give you something that I thought you should have."

I try to follow his story, but I am confused and it seems to me that everything is taking place far away from me: I am not the protagonist but only a spectator. How could I not understand, at least from the surname, that this man was part of my family? Was it because I was shaken by the many events that have taken place in this period, inside and outside the four walls of my home?

Alex doesn't dare to look him in the eye, he is curled up in a chair and, most of the time, keeps his head down. My brother suffered more. He, who could not ask our mother any questions when dad left, he, who immersed himself in complete silence, transforming himself into a wild and arrogant person, he who succumbed to vices, losing himself.

Suddenly Andy interrupts the story and stands up, goes out and calls the boy who accompanied him earlier. He looks like a photocopy of him, but at a young age. "This is Benny, my son and ... your stepbrother." Then he turns to him: "Show them what's in the boxes."

He comes near and greets us warmly. We feel numb; everything is happening so fast that we can't really process the emotions all at once.

"These are the letters I sent to Elena when I was young and was crazy for her. They are the fiery feelings of a boy ready to do everything in the name of love. We were the most beautiful couple in the city. While here are the ones I wrote in Greece and one is from a few days ago. I didn't have the courage to send them and, later, when you left Albania, I did not have your address. They helped me to survive. Often the feelings of guilt were so strong that they nearly killed me. But now ... I don't know how many more years I have to live and I don't need them anymore; they now belong to you. They will help you understand that love is not only about passion and sentiment, but also error and madness."

I take the boxes in my hands and caress them. They are now my greatest treasure.

A JOURNEY TO HEAVEN

Mom, this is your last journey, from which you will never return: the journey to rest in your land, which you loved very much, even if it gave you few joys and so much suffering.

"You never forget your land, you take its memory with you, even if you go to the end of the world," so you told me.

I want to think that you are now going towards a better, more peaceful world, where there are no quarrels, betrayals, abandonments, where everyone is calm and happy. I want to think that you will rest in a place where there is no darkness, sadness, diseases, but only sun and light.

Today I am with Alex, my strong yet fragile brother. He admitted to me that he had made many mistakes, but now he is a different person, he has found his way, the one you wanted: straight, without traps and adventures.

We are getting to know each other, as we have never done before, and for this, your memory, your love, is helping us. We think about you every day, Mom. As from an ancient casket we bring out the conversations, your jokes, your positivity, and all of these relieve us of the pain.

I have someone close, whom you loved and waited for until the last moments: your husband, our father. Anton. We met him today, for the first time. Perhaps, God brought him to us in these very difficult moments to fill the void left by your disappearance. This red carnation that he brought you from afar is a symbol of the love he has nurtured for you until today. He has never forgotten you, he wrote you a letter every day, without finding the courage or the possibility to send them. But you probably knew it, you felt it, even if life proved to be stingy and didn't give you another chance to see each other.

"It's nice to forgive someone for the mistakes he has made, because you feel your soul as light as a feather," you once said to me.

That's what Alex and I did with each other, and also with dad.

I wanted to share with you some good news that you have dreamed more than me. A child is growing inside me who, in a short time, has been able to change my way of thinking and living. My theories, of being free and enjoying life, have evaporated. Maybe in this respect I was like dad. He too idealized freedom, but now he says that his happiness are us, his children.

This creature is a gift of love for Diego, whom I truly discovered in this dark and difficult period. It is a gift for you who was hoping to have a grandchild but, above all, for me, who realized how much I need to pass on to someone those teachings and values that you have handed to us over the years.

I want this creature to resemble you, Mom, with the love you had for people and for life itself. I hope you will watch us from up there, while my daughter and I will run in the green parks and you will rejoice with us.

Have a good journey to heaven, dear mom!

Bergamo, June 2020

THE AUTHOR

Irma Kurti is an Albanian poetess, writer, lyricist, journalist, and translator. She is a naturalized Italian. She has been writing since she was a child. In 1980, she was honored with the first national prize on the 35th anniversary of the *Pionieri* magazine for her poem "To my homeland". In 1989, she won the second prize in the National Competition organized by Radio Tirana on the 45th anniversary of the Liberation of Albania.

All her books are dedicated to the memory of her beloved parents Hasan Kurti and Sherife Mezini, who supported and encouraged every step of her literary path.

Kurti has won numerous literary prizes and awards in Italy and Italian Switzerland. She was awarded the "Universum Donna" International Prize IX Edition 2013 for Literature and the lifetime nomination of "Ambassador of Peace" by the University of Peace of Italian Switzerland. In 2020, she received the title of Honorary President of WikiPoesia, the Encyclopedia of Poetry.

In 2021, she was awarded the title "Liria" (Freedom) by the Arbëreshë Community in Italy.

Irma Kurti has published 25 books in Albanian, 17 in Italian and 6 in English. She has written about 150 lyrics for adults and children, including in Italian and English. She lives in Bergamo, Italy.

www.ingramcontent.com/pod-product-compliance
Lightning Source LLC
LaVergne TN
LVHW041023150826
845672LV00001B/183
9786214701773